WAR OF THE ROSE COVENS

Published by Clockwork Dragon, LLC
www.clockworkdragon.net

First Printing, June 2019

War of the Rose Covens is a work of fiction sited in a fictional version of the Pacific Northwest. People, places, and incidents are either products of the author's mind or used fictitiously. No endorsement of any kind should be inferred by existing locations or organizations within it.

No teenagers, rosebushes, displaced gods, or witches were harmed in the making of this book.

ISBN: 978-1-944334-41-3

WAR OF THE ROSE COVENS

LEE FRENCH

a Spirit Knights novel

For Erik, who demanded this book.

For Connie, who keeps my head on straight.

For Marguerite, who smacked my indecision into decision.

For Jonathan, who is generally awesome in every way.

For James, who said the right thing at the right time.

For the Rebel Writers, who make me laugh on a regular basis and give me an excuse to eat terrible things for breakfast once in a while.

CHAPTER 1

Blue-tinted magic, strong enough for me to see without trying, cocooned my house. As usual. Fat, fluffy flakes drifted out of the morning sky. The snow melted where it touched the road and the driveway. An inch-thick layer of white covered the grass and clung to the trees and the bare canes of my mother's prize-winning rosebushes. Above the driveway, black plastic covered my destroyed bedroom window, held in place by silver duct tape.

A week ago, on Christmas Day, I left with friends to go save the city. They'd smashed my bedroom window to get me out. Mom had said not to bother coming back. Until now, I hadn't.

New year, fresh start. School started again tomorrow, so I at least needed my backpack. Which put me on the front porch, working up the nerve to ring the doorbell. Some people might walk right in, I thought, but not me.

I stared at the door, piecing together my worst-case scenario. Mom could answer the door and spray magic in my face. Dad could answer the door and look at me like I'd murdered his puppy. My brothers answering the door didn't seem bad.

Wait, no, Mom could answer the door and want to talk about my decision to leave the Petal Society coven at length and in detail. That sounded much worse than anything else.

Either I rang the bell or I didn't. Two choices. One left everything unresolved. The other sucked.

With a sigh, I stared at the door for another few seconds. My family mattered. I could get a new one, so to speak, but I needed to try with the one I already had. They'd been fine until I met Drew.

Drew, a boy my age and one of those friends who broke the window, had needed help. I'd done what I could.

I reached out and pushed the doorbell. *Ding-dong.* My belly churned.

Too soon, Mom opened the door. Her strong blue aura flared in my face as if to fill the space around me and make up for my weakness.

For three long heartbeats that stretched into forever, we stared at each other. Her blonde hair, the same shade of light yellow as mine, hung to her shoulders, ending with thick, fake curls. The tiny lines at the corners of her blue eyes seemed more tense and tight than usual.

Mom lunged and wrapped her arms around me. She held me tighter than I remembered her ever hugging me before.

"I was so worried!"

Still wary of what might come next, I returned the hug and waited.

Mom let go and herded me inside. Her warding on the house rippled across my skin and clamped down on my meager abilities. She'd removed me from the protections. Maybe she'd done it in anger right after I left. Once done, she wouldn't have been able to add me again without my presence.

"Where have you been staying? Are you hungry?" She stopped in front of the couch in the living room and pressed on my shoulders to make me sit with her.

I didn't resist. In her house, suppressed by her magic, I had few choices. "I'm fine."

She held my chin and made me look at her. "You're not fine. There's something off about your aura."

Not sure what to say, I shrugged. My aura had a link to Drew, and we'd formed a coven together. Mom could read auras better than anyone else

I knew, so she'd see it.

Mom frowned. "What have you been doing?"

Saving the world. I didn't say it because it sounded ridiculous. "Helping my friends."

"More like letting them help themselves to you," Mom muttered. She scowled at me. "This is about that boy."

I wanted to roll my eyes but didn't. Not with Mom staring me in the face. "His name is Drew."

Abandoning me on the couch, Mom stood and paced. "If your father was here, he'd tan your hide for letting some boy take advantage of you. Lucky for you, he left with your brothers already."

Until Mom mentioned it, I hadn't realized how much I regretted missing our annual New Year's hike. Every year, we packed lunches and spent the day in a giant park. Last year, we'd gone to Multnomah Falls. This year, he'd talked about Mount Hood. When Mount St. Helens had erupted a few days before Christmas, he'd reconsidered and suggested someplace south of Portland instead.

"We can still handle this," Mom continued. "I know you were upset on Christmas. I was too! But we can fix everything now. You can rejoin the coven and never see that boy again. It'll be like nothing happened."

"But I don't—"

"Hush. I know that seems hard." Mom patted me on the head. "I'll sponsor you again. No one will bat an eye. You're a teenager. Teenagers sometimes do rash things, and we all know that. We can go tomorrow, after school."

"Mom, I just—"

"Don't worry about any of it. I'll take care of everything." She turned her back on me and left the room. "Do you want some juice?"

"No." I huffed and stood. Nothing had changed. Strike that—one thing had changed. I now knew I deserved better than a mom who couldn't believe I'd aged past twelve. I had friends, and I had another group of people willing to take me in, so I didn't have to stay at home.

I rushed upstairs to my bedroom. If I had to leave, I wanted to take some of my stuff. My pink backpack hung on the chair at my white desk. Yanking it off the chair, I surveyed the room. Next to a picture of Mom and me, I had one of the coven. All the women in it were related to me one way or another. Another showed me with my cousin Ashley, my best friend.

Leaving the coven meant leaving Ashley behind.

Staring at the photo, I tried to decide if I wanted to take it or not. Her mom had snapped it last summer, on our shared sixteenth birthday. We wore glitter-covered party hats and grinned for the camera with fresh, expert-level makeup. Mom and Aunt Mimi had taken us to a fancy salon where they gave us the works.

I'd known Ashley all my life. We called ourselves twins. Maybe I should've gone to see her first, but coming home had seemed more important.

"What are you doing with your backpack?"

Startled, I spun to find Mom in my doorway, one hand on her hip, the other holding a plastic cup. Probably, it held the juice I'd said I didn't want. She scowled again.

Unable to tell her the truth for no reason I knew, I looked at the strap over my shoulder. "Holding it."

The muscles around her mouth twitched. She didn't like the answer. "You're too old for a security blanket, even if it is a backpack."

Her unspoken command made my shoulders tense. I set the pack on my chair.

"Now have a seat." Mom waved at the bed. "Drink some juice while I break these odd links to your aura."

I froze. Other people couldn't break a coven link. Mom had taught me that. Had she lied?

"Sit." Mom shoved the cup into my hand and pointed at the edge of my bed.

My gaze followed her finger. More tension bunched at the base of my skull. If I sat, she'd do everything in her power to break my links with Drew. I didn't want that. He'd done some stupid crap, but had never hurt me on purpose. He tried to be kind and supportive, even if he sometimes failed.

We'd linked our auras and formed a coven for a reason. No matter what my mom thought, it was a good reason.

One week ago, I'd faced the most powerful witch-ghost-thing imaginable and lived to tell about it. Drew and a bunch of other people had done most of the work, but I'd helped stop it from devouring the entire world.

My mom scared me a lot more.

I hesitated.

"Sophie." Mom used her stern voice. Her aura flared. Magic wrapped around me in a suffocating embrace and shoved me toward the bed. "Sit down."

Compared to Mom's blazing sun of witch power, I nursed a tiny candle flame of disappointment. Through my link with Drew, I could overcome that. If she hadn't removed me from the house's protections, that is. Under the restraints of her warding, I had no chance of resisting her.

My body sat on the edge of my pink bedspread. I opened my mouth to complain. Pressure snapped my jaws shut.

"No backtalk," Mom said, her words clipped. She sat beside me and took my hand.

Her power flooded over me. I drowned in an overwhelming wave.

In that unbearable moment, I hated her. Four years ago, she'd forced my latent witch power awake and found the result disappointing. Now she forced my aura clean because she didn't approve of my choices.

At least, she tried to force those links to break. I imagined myself holding the focus stone I wore under my shirt. Using it helped me concentrate and direct power better. Then I created a mental picture of my link with Drew. It looked like a shining, sky blue cord. Still gripping the focus stone with one mental hand, I used the other to grab the cord and wrap it around my arm.

Mom could clamp down on my body and my power, but she couldn't stop me from protecting my own aura.

CHAPTER 2

I stood inside a small cabin by myself. Entering a metaphysical space, something I'd done a few times before, meant Mom's power had forced us into a sort of duel. That alone made me cheer. Before I linked with Drew, I couldn't have caused this. His power fed into mine like a battery, giving me enough to resist Mom.

She'd be furious when this ended, no matter what happened.

The cabin had a wide bed, big enough for three people, with green sheets. Living trees sculpted by magic formed the walls, though all the wood looked gray and brittle. Hundreds of dead leaves hung in curtains and covered the bed like sheets. The cabin had no windows and only one door. A single flimsy latch held the door shut.

Two sky blue tokens lay on the bed. One represented the aura link between Drew and me. I could tell without touching it. The other marked my coven allegiance. Since I'd never been in a metaphysical battle for my own mind, I'd never seen the old token, the one that had bound me to the Petal Society. This new one had a silver outline of a dragon burned into it.

My surroundings surprised me. Somehow, the place I'd stayed for the past week felt more like a home to me than the house where my family lived. Because I wouldn't have conjured any other space than the one where my heart belonged.

Everyone there, a big family of people who cared about each other, accepted me as another daughter and sister. Except Drew, because he and I had a...complicated relationship due to the aura meshing. His girlfriend, Claire, and I got along well, which made things less weird.

The front door rattled. I threw my back against it to hold it shut. At some point, I needed to work on the lock. That pathetic piece of metal represented my passive defenses.

"Sophie?" The wood muffled Mom's voice enough to let me know she wouldn't hear me unless I wanted it or shouted. "Are you in there?"

Like an obedient little girl, I opened my mouth to answer. But I stopped before I said anything. She had no right to attack my link with Drew or to dissolve our coven. I'd made those choices for good reasons.

The door rattled again.

In this space, every action we took relied on two things—power and force of will. Whoever wanted something harder and had the magical reservoir to back it up would win. I had to want my links and privacy more than Mom wanted to enforce her will over me.

"Sophie, sweetie, this is for your own good. You don't understand what you've done. These things have repercussions. You've made ripples that you can't unmake. Without the coven, you're unprotected."

I wanted to listen to her. I wanted to believe she knew better. How many times had she told me as much? I needed supervision. I couldn't do anything except the bare minimum. I'd turned out pathetic and useless, but no one else had, ever, in the entire history of the bloodline.

"Open the door, Sophie."

So long as I kept my mouth shut, she might believe I had no control over this.

The door rattled again, this time harder. I braced my feet on the foot of the bed. If she broke in, not only would she break the links I'd forged on purpose, she'd see where I'd been staying for the past week. The explanation would take too much from me.

"Sophie, I'm giving you one last chance. Open this door right now or

I'll break it down." Her stern voice goaded me to give up. Roll over and lie down, be a good girl, and let Mom do what she wants. "You know you can't hold it against me. You don't have enough power. You never have, and you never will. I don't want to hurt you. If you make me, I will."

I covered my face with both hands. Eventually, Mom would break through, and I couldn't do anything about that.

"I take it the reunion is going poorly," Drew said.

Opening my eyes, I snapped my head to the side and saw him standing beside me. Curly red hair framed a freckled face with black-rimmed glasses, like always. A black tattoo of roses covered the right side of his face. He grinned like he found the situation funny.

"Keep your voice down," I said in a harsh whisper. "She can hear us."

"Sorry." He scanned the room. "Why are we here?"

"Mom wants to break the links between us. She thinks you're a bad influence or something."

Drew stared at me.

The door thumped hard enough to shove me. I rebounded and pressed my back against it again.

"Wait." Drew leaned against the door with me. "This is your inner psyche? I'm inside your private mental sanctum thingy?"

I wanted to slap him for acting dumb, except he knew even less about how magic worked than I did. At least his presence gave me a backbone. Resisting Mom seemed easier with him by my side. "Yes. Mom is trying to get in so she can see everything and break the links. She thinks my connections to you are because I'm a stupid, lovesick teenager."

"Someone breaking into your private mental sanctum thingy sounds bad."

Thank you, Captain Obvious. "Yeah. It's bad. It'll hurt. And among other things, she'll find out where I've been for the past week." That ranked low on my list of priorities for things I didn't want Mom to know, but I knew he'd latch onto it.

The door banged hard enough to shove us both an inch.

"Your defenses kind of suck." Drew leaned past me to examine the latch. "I stand corrected. They really suck a lot. So, repel her for now, then we're going to work on shoring up this space. Since I think repelling her will toss me out, my suggestion is that you leave the house as soon as possible afterward."

"I can't just leave my family. I came back for a reason."

"If you stay, she'll probably try to catch you off guard at some later point. Like in your sleep. This attack proves you can't trust her until she respects you."

His words hit home. Trust and respect—two things I'd never gotten from my family or coven. Drew gave me both, freely and without hesitation. So did Claire and the rest of the family I'd fallen into.

"Okay, but I'm not giving up on them."

"That's fine. Let's focus on getting through this now and deal with the rest later." He held up his hand.

I took his hand and squeezed it. "Do you know how to repel an attack on a sanctum? Because I don't."

"Not really." He scanned the room again. "Is the door definitely the only way she can get in?"

"Yes. The door is a metaphor for gaining entry. Everything else is a metaphor for the anchor connecting my aura to me."

"Because metaphysical stuff is always a metaphor. Right." Drew pointed to the two stones. "And she wants to get those and destroy them, right?" When I nodded, he let go of me and the door to scoop up both stones and tuck them into his pocket. "That should make them harder to get if she somehow breaks through."

I wanted to object because that didn't make any sense. He couldn't take the manifestation of my connection to him and hide it in his own psyche. Unless he could. Drew did seem to operate as an exception to every rule I knew about magic.

Whatever. "The next step is probably doing something to the door."

Drew patted his pocket and rejoined me in blocking the door. "You told me that magic is about nurturing and life. Growing. That kind of thing. How do we use that here?"

The whole cabin shook. All the leaves fluttered and bounced with a dry, raspy crackle.

"Sophie!" Mom screamed. "You open this door right now or you'll be sorry!"

"Every time I meet your mom, she's just so nice and welcoming."

I scowled. He smiled. Boys.

The door rattled so hard it made my teeth chatter. Out of the corner of my eye, I saw the latch jiggle. I turned and gulped. Both screws holding the hook on the wall hung halfway out of the latch plate.

Resigned to failure, I sighed. "If she gets the door open, you should leave. I don't want her to get those two tokens. I don't even want her to see you here."

"Let's hope it doesn't come to that."

It would. I knew in my heart it would.

The door bounced us again. One screw popped out of the latch plate. The other would only take one more solid blow.

Drew turned and shoved his shoulder against the door. "I'm trying to pour power into the door, to make it grow enough to wedge itself into the frame, but nothing is happening."

"The warding on the house. It has to be constraining us." I hung my head and rubbed my eyes.

"She's going to get through."

"Yeah." And it would suck.

"I'll get you out."

"No." I shook my head and wished I could let him rescue me. "She'll be so much worse if you come and assault her wards. Just let me deal with this, okay?"

He laid a hand on my shoulder and squeezed. "I don't want to abandon you."

"I know." I couldn't look him in the eye. "But you can't rescue me from my family. I have to fix this, and you'll hinder more than help."

We held the door against another rattling assault.

Drew looked past me to the latch. "I'm sorry. When you need me, call."

"You don't have a phone."

We gave each other weak smiles. He leaned close and kissed my cheek, then he disappeared.

The door slammed open. It threw me aside. My head cracked against the wall.

CHAPTER 3

Mom wouldn't leave, and I couldn't stop crying. She kept rubbing my back. Every moment in contact with her felt worse than the last. I wanted to throw up.

Once she'd broken through, she'd torn the cabin apart looking for the tokens. Nothing had stayed safe from her. If she'd wanted to know everything, she could've learned it all. With her obsessive focus on the tokens, at least she still didn't know much.

"I know you're upset, sweetie. But you shouldn't have resisted me. I warned you. And now here we are. It didn't even work, so we'll have to do it again. And since it didn't work, you're obviously hiding things from me, which isn't acceptable. You're grounded until the end of the month. I'll take you to school and pick you up afterward, and you can't leave the house without me."

Finally, she took her hand off me and stood. "If Drew comes here again, I'll deal with him like I would anyone else who's hurt my little girl." She turned on her heel and stalked out of my bedroom.

My head hurt too much to care. Mom had broken into me and ripped me apart. I felt the same as when she'd forced open my aura to give me witch powers. Used. Violated. Broken. Four years after she'd done that, I thought I'd grown past it.

I thought I could handle it.

I cried into my pillow with wild, hysterical sobbing. Why had I thought I could talk to Mom? She didn't understand anything. When she looked at me, she saw a disaster zone. No decision I made for myself could ever be right.

"Oh, Sophie." Mom sighed. I didn't check, but she sounded like she stood in my doorway. "There's really nothing to be so upset about. How about if I invite some of your friends to come over today? We can have a nice lunch with a full house."

On the giant list of things I wanted, seeing whoever my mom wanted to invite for lunch ranked below visiting the dentist. At least the dentist cleaned my teeth. Her idea of "my friends" would make everything worse. I didn't even want to see Ashley.

I didn't know what I did want.

That was a lie.

I wanted Drew to come and soothe my aura. Since it didn't happen automatically, I knew the wards blocked him from helping. He probably couldn't even feel anything wrong with me. The metaphysical space of my private sanctum had used a loophole. In the real world, we had no functional connection through the wards.

"I'll take your silence as a yes. Get up and get ready."

As soon as she left, I poured my pain into the pillow. At some point, I lifted my head and wiped my face. Every inch of my body ached, inside and out. I could take some painkillers and smile at everyone as if nothing had happened. Mom would like that.

Wind ruffled the plastic sheeting over the hole in my wall. On the edge of my vision, I could see the ripple of magic from Mom's warding. The warding had never prevented me from leaving the house before, and I doubted Mom had changed that. With her decision to ground me, she might consider updating it.

If I wanted to leave, I had two options. One, I could wait a month until Mom relaxed the wards and let me out of her sight for five seconds.

Two, I could suck it up and run before she had a chance to change anything.

Leaving now probably meant leaving for good. The next time I tried to come back, Mom wouldn't give me smiles and sunshine. We'd fight, and it would hurt both of us.

Unless I could convince some of the other coven members to help? Two of my aunts, Anne and Stace, had been there when I renounced the coven. They knew what had happened, and they both knew Drew. Neither would attack me. If I asked as a member of the family, one or both might talk to Mom for me.

The rush of a concrete plan shoved all my pain aside. I lurched off the bed and shut my bedroom door. Locking it wouldn't stop Mom, but it would slow her down, so I did that. I scrambled to find the things I needed most—clothes, money, and school stuff. Spending as little time as possible, I snagged whatever I could find, stuffed it all into my backpack, and climbed onto my desk.

As soon as I crossed the plane of the warding, Mom would know. Crouching on my desk, I visualized punching through and tearing open the plastic. It wouldn't work. My muscles didn't only hurt, they had no real strength. Nice girls didn't lift weights, they did aerobics. According to Mom.

Plastic would defeat me. Of all the things to get into my way, this one seemed like a terrible insult.

Wait. I had scissors. My desk drawer had all kinds of things. I yanked it open and pawed through pencils, pens, erasers, and more to find a pair of scissors. With them open, I took a deep breath.

This act was final. Once I stabbed through the wards and plastic, I couldn't take it back.

I turned to see the door. How many times had Mom or Dad come to help me with homework or wish me good night? My little brothers had never done anything wrong. What if my leaving meant something bad happened to them?

But I had to save myself. Mom would keep destroying me until she figured out how to break those links. I couldn't take that again. With the tokens in Drew's hands, she'd do it over and over until she killed me.

Later, I could come check on my brothers. Drew would help me do it.

Turning my back on the door, I squared my shoulders. I could do this.

Someone knocked on my door. My chest exploded with panic. "Sophie, your friends will be here soon. Are you getting ready?"

"Yes, Mom." Could she hear the hitch in my voice?

"If you're changing clothes, you might consider a dress for Gabe. He likes you."

"Okay." Part of me yearned to obey. Put on makeup. Wear a dress. Style my hair. Smile. Laugh at jokes. Pretend I cared.

The last boy I thought I liked had betrayed me the first moment he could. As if I would open myself to that possibility again with someone Mom shoved at me. Not that I hated Gabe. He wanted to date me and said all the right things. The guy had that tall, dark, and handsome thing going on, with just enough athleticism to sweep most girls off their feet.

But I wanted a friend, not a boyfriend.

"Don't take too long. I want you downstairs when everyone gets here."

"Yes, Mom."

I heard the floor creak as she walked away.

I could do this. I could do this. I could do this.

As soon as I heard the distant, muffled squeak from the bottom stair, I took a deep breath and stabbed the plastic. My scissors sliced open a hole. I shoved my body through it and gasped at the frigid air. I'd left my coat downstairs, so I wore three sweaters, which didn't keep me warm enough.

Soothing magic flowed into my aura. I'd half-feared Mom had somehow broken the link without realizing it. Relief washed over me as much as Drew's power. With his backing, I could resist Mom. She couldn't drag me inside again. Not without knocking me unconscious.

Scrambling across the icy roof as fast as I dared, I focused on my hands and feet. Mom would come running, I figured. She'd have to climb the stairs again, then break through the locked door.

Never mind her. I reached the corner with a tall juniper and wrapped bands of power around it. The branches reached for me. I jumped into them. Under my command, the plant set me on my feet.

"Sophie!"

Unable to resist the tone of her voice, I froze and turned to see her. Mom had gone to the front door instead of my room. She stood on the porch. Her aura blazed bright enough that I could see it without trying.

She glared at me. "Come back now and I'll overlook this."

No, she wouldn't. This choice had been made. Going back now meant worse than I'd already endured. It meant giving up and giving in again. I'd done that for the last time.

I ran down the driveway.

CHAPTER 4

A car stopped two feet in front of me with a squeal of brakes. I panicked. The driver and I made eye contact. Gabriel Avenatti, the very guy I didn't want to see at the moment, had come at Mom's call.

He blinked at me, his dark eyes wide and dilated from almost killing me with his car. I tried and failed to breathe. Wild fantasies popped into my head, of him leaping out of his car to tower over Mom and intimidate her into submission with his muscles.

Not that I thought he would do it.

Could I trust Gabe? I didn't know. He'd come when Mom called, and I knew he wanted to date me. On the other hand, if Drew hadn't waited for me across the street, I didn't have a serious escape plan.

"Sophie!" Mom's voice carried a dark, deep echo.

I felt her power surge over me. Thick arms of magical power slammed into me. Drew's energy bolstered my pathetic aura, providing more than enough of a defense.

Cracking like thunder boomed from the front door. I turned and saw Mom hit the ground, her eyes wide with shock. Paralyzed by the sight, I watched her lift her head and shake it.

What had I done? My mother wanted to protect me. She had a stupid idea of how to do that, but if she would listen for five minutes, I knew—

The fuzziness drained from her face. She locked her gaze on me. Rage burned in her snarl and her glare.

Terrified of her, I took a step back.

"Get in," Gabe said through the open passenger-side window.

I dove into the window head-first. The car backed out of the driveway before I pulled in my legs. Gabe gave me a hand, helping me get into the seat while also tearing down the street at Mach 5. He said nothing as I checked on Mom. She ran to the end of the driveway with lightning crackling around her body.

We turned down the next street.

"Are you okay?"

Was I okay? No, I was not okay. I covered my face and doubled over. My entire body shook. High-pitched, hysterical noises blurted out of my mouth.

"This wasn't what I expected," Drew said.

Gabe slammed on the brakes. I hit the dashboard and crumpled into a gibbering pile of uselessness on the floorboards. The boys shouted at each other.

"Go!" I screamed at Gabe. "He's with me!"

The car moved again. No one said anything. I hugged myself. When I stopped shaking, I climbed into the seat again.

Gabe kept his eyes on the road as he drove us farther and farther from my house. He and Drew had nothing in common other than their grade level. Skinny, redheaded Drew played chess. Brawny, tanned Gabe played soccer and ran track.

Both had leaped to my defense. I smelled the potential for trouble between them.

"Thank you."

Nodding, Gabe glanced at me. "Are you okay now?"

I didn't have an answer yet.

"She tried to swat you." Drew reached between the front seats.

Not sure what he wanted or offered, I touched his hand. His power had already soothed my aura. The contact soothed something else, something deeper and more intimate. Hungry for that comfort, I gripped his hand.

"Swat how?" Gabe glanced at our hands. I couldn't translate the fleeting look. He'd asked me out at least fifty times since I started my freshman year, so I had a solid guess.

"With magic."

Drew squeezed my hand. "He knows?"

"He knows enough." I hadn't ever explained anything magical to Gabe, but he had some rudimentary understanding of it. Like Drew, he carried the potential to use magic and would pass that on if he ever had kids. Unlike Drew, no one had forced his potential active and awake.

"He's heard some stories," Gabe said as he flicked his gaze to the rearview mirror, "and seen some things."

"Cool," Drew said. "Do you want me to take you home?"

Gabe braked hard to avoid hitting the car in front of us, stopped at a red light. "After what just happened? Are you crazy?"

"He means somewhere else." The home with that cabin sounded nice. Except for all the people. As much as I adored Claire's family, I didn't think I could handle that many well-meaning attempts to cheer me up or declarations of anger at my mom. "Not right now. I need to...I don't know."

Drew squeezed my hand again. He knew the extent of what I'd endured today even if he didn't know how it felt. "Where would you like to go?"

"I kind of need to know that too," Gabe said.

"We could get ice cream," Drew said. "No, wait. It's kind of cold for that. Hot cocoa? A pastry?"

I couldn't help letting a smile ghost at the corners of my mouth. He sounded like a puppy trying desperately to please his master.

"I need to go see Aunt Stace."

Drew raised his brow. "Interesting choice. You don't think she'll try to reel you back into the coven?"

"Wait, you left the coven?"

Both Drew and I blinked at Gabe.

"Yes, about a week ago."

Gabe let out a relieved sigh. "Oh, thank God. I can finally stop with this crap. He stopped at another red light and turned to face me. "Sophie, I don't want to date you. I've never wanted to date you. Which isn't anything against you. I'm gay, and I've known since I was ten."

The tension in the car broke with an almost audible snap. I stared at him. Then I giggled. My giggles degraded into mad, lunatic laughter. Still clutching Drew's hand like a lifeline, I gasped and wheezed and snorted and cried.

The boys introduced themselves to each other while I struggled to regain some level of control over myself. They spoke for a minute or two, then stopped while I sobbed into my sweaters. At some point, Drew tugged on my hand like he wanted me to climb into the back seat, so I did. I curled in his lap and let him hold me.

"So you guys are a thing?" Gabe asked.

"Not really?" Drew rubbed circles on my back like my mom had. He provided actual comfort and didn't make me want to barf. "I have a girlfriend."

Claire wouldn't have let anyone invade her private sanctum. She would've stood firm and punched Mom in the face. At least, that sounded like something she would do. I wished I had that much courage. Instead, I smeared my snot and tears all over Drew's jacket.

"You look like a thing."

"It's complicated. Why did you pretend like you wanted to date Sophie?"

By this point, I'd calmed enough to listen to them through my sniffles and random hiccups. Talking felt like too much effort.

Gabe shifted in his seat. "My mom is a member of the Rose Quarter coven."

Rivals with the Petal Society for as long as both had existed, the Rose Quarter witches competed with us over anything and everything related to Portland's Rose Festival and its parade. Both covens grasped and scrabbled for first prize in every available category.

My jaw fell open. "You wanted to spy on us by dating me?"

"Them," Drew murmured.

Yes, I needed to remember I no longer belonged to the Petal Society. Or my mom. I belonged to Drew and Claire.

Gabe squirmed and glanced out the side window, avoiding using his mirrors. "I didn't want to do it."

Drew and I both watched him and waited for more.

"Did they threaten to shove you out of the closet?" Drew asked.

"I wish." Gabe shook his head. "I would much rather be out and dating guys instead of griping to myself in secret. No, they threatened something much worse. Date Sophie of my own free will or they'll make me do it through a magical compulsion. My mom is pretty hardcore about the whole serving the family thing. I mean, I'm just a boy. Boys are for breeding so we can get more witches." By the end, he sounded bitter enough for the both of us.

"Wow." Drew knew a thing or two about magical compulsions. He'd endured a lot before I met him.

"That's just wrong." As if my mom hadn't done things at least as bad to me. "Why do they all have to be so..." I groped for the right word.

"Controlling? Obsessive?" Gabe sighed. "Maybe it's a witch thing."

"I don't feel a need to control anyone," Drew said.

"You're a guy, not a witch. Boys can't be witches."

Drew laughed. "And yet, I'm a witch."

I didn't want to talk about that. "It's a long story, and it doesn't matter. I'm a witch, and I don't want to control anyone."

The car stopped. I saw nothing but trees from my angle.

"We're here," Gabe said. "Are you sure this is a good idea?"

"I don't think there are any good options right now." Drew helped me sit up. "This one happens to not involve her mom."

We'd arrived at Aunt Stace's house in Hillsboro. Like I'd said I wanted.

At least they listened to me.

CHAPTER 5

Stace's house squatted in a small clearing surrounded by giant cedars and sycamores. The log cabin style cottage featured brown trim and leafy green accents with whimsical whorls and curves, as if Stace wanted people to mistake her home for undecorated gingerbread.

Gabe had stopped on the road, so I could see Stace's bright red mailbox perched on a post. Another car sat on the narrow gravel driveway. I recognized it as belonging to another member of the Petal Society, Anne. She and I had a common ancestor five or six generations back.

Stace, for the record, wasn't really my aunt. Her mom was my great-grandmother's niece. Or something like that. Everyone in the coven could trace her lineage to Jacqueline Whidby or her daughter, Sophie, which made us all cousins of one remove or another.

I didn't have any actual aunts in the area because my mom's only sibling, her younger sister Jennifer, had died at the age of twelve. How she'd died, I had no idea. No one would talk about it except to mention how much she'd liked roses. Unspeakable tragedy seemed likely.

My dad's family all lived on the East Coast. We didn't see them much. As far as I knew, they had no witches.

"Maybe you guys should stay in the car." I didn't want to let go of Drew, but I didn't see anything going well with him inside. The coven didn't like him much for being an abomination of a witch. Events with that witch-ghost-thing had put friction between him, Anne, and Stace. And once they found out about Gabe, Anne and Stace would want details and try to wheedle dirt for the coven.

Anything and everything for the coven. Always.

"This is really my problem," I said.

"I can see how we'd just complicate things." Drew opened the door for me. "We'll go wait someplace else. Tug on the line when you're ready to leave."

I stepped out. Drew kissed my cheek. Warmed by his affection, I watched as he shut the door and Gabe drove the car up the road.

Stace's house had never struck me as sinister before. I shivered, wishing I had a coat and knowing it wouldn't help much. Standing on the side of the road wouldn't solve anything, so I forced myself to trudge to the door.

As I had at my own home, I hesitated on the front stoop.

The place where my mom lived didn't deserve that label from me anymore. I'd seen where I hung my heart and knew where I wanted to live. With Drew and Claire, I had plenty of family and plenty of people who believed in me.

I entertained the idea of leaving and not bothering to deal with the coven or my family anymore. In time, Mom might mellow. If I stayed away for the rest of the school year, she might see me in a different light.

Without me to take the brunt of her, what would she do to my brothers? Would she latch onto another girl in the family? Someone needed to keep her occupied.

The door opened. I hadn't knocked and didn't know what to say yet.

Stace stood in the doorway. Her brown hair had more gray than I remembered, and she seemed to droop in her faded, tie-dye dress. Every wrinkle on her face and neck stood out, as if she'd stretched her skin and let it fall back into place.

"Are you going to knock or just stand out here for a while?" She sounded raspy and dry, like old paper crumpling.

"I..." I stared at her, not sure what to say.

"I know how you feel." Stace offered me a hand. "Come in, have some tea with us."

I took her hand and stepped inside.

Anne sat in the warm room, on one of the wood benches grown from the trees Stace had used to create her house. She and Stace had the same sort of feel about them, of earthy, middle-aged women who wanted to have tea, grow gardens, and bake cookies. Anne favored more muted colors and wore a pair of glasses on a beaded necklace. She also had about fifteen fewer years behind her. Today, I could see it in stark contrast with Stace, especially around the eyes.

Stowing her phone in a pocket, Anne patted the bench for me to sit beside her. "How are you, Sophie?"

"Fine." I sat beside her like an obedient dog.

"Your aura seems a bit unsettled," Anne said.

Mom was the expert, but every single witch I knew could see auras without trying. Not me. Of course not me. Sometimes, I caught one out of the corner of my eye when I knew to look for it, like with the wards at Mom's house. Most of the time, I saw nothing unless I made an effort on purpose. Except that I could always see Drew's aura.

"Yeah." The fresh memory of Mom's assault made me hug myself. I would've liked some warmth from one of them, but they didn't offer.

"Why are you here?" Stace sounded like she wanted me to leave. Like I wasn't welcome.

I leaned forward and held my head with both hands. "I tried to go home."

After a long pause, Anne said, "And?"

"Mom tried to break my links to Drew so she could bring me back into the coven."

Both women stayed quiet for so long that I lifted my head. They watched me like I had cooties.

Stace shrugged. "And?"

"And?" I'd come to the wrong place, apparently. "And she broke into my psyche! She tried to rearrange my aura to suit herself!"

Anne and Stace glanced at each other.

Patting my shoulder, Anne said, "It doesn't hurt if you don't resist."

I yanked away and stood. "That makes it okay?"

"You're sixteen, Sophie." Stace held up her hands in surrender. "She's your mother. Until you're an adult, she has the right to do whatever she thinks is best for you. If that means breaking your link to Drew, we're not going to stop her."

The stab of betrayal lodged in my gut. Again. Mom had done it, and now Stace and Anne. I'd trusted them all, and they used me.

For a purpose? Did they need me in the coven for some reason? Did they need me alone and incapable? Nothing ever revolved around me, and I'd gotten used to that. Always the bridesmaid, never the bride, the saying went. Between Ashley and me, she always got the better grades, always did the cooler things, and always had the nicer stuff. The coven fawned over her, and so did all the boys.

I was the pretty girl's friend—in the coven and at school.

But what if they needed me for something? What if they had something going on and needed a sacrifice or a conduit?

What if Mom had taken her disappointment in me and wrapped that up with a fancy bow so she could justify using me for some purpose? After all, she still had two sons. Maybe she considered her pathetic daughter an acceptable loss.

"You should go home," Anne said. "I know things seem hard right now, but give it more time."

"I'm grounded to infinity," I grumbled.

Stace stood and held her arms open like she expected me to hug her. I recoiled and stepped closer to the front door. She sighed and lowered her arms.

"I have an idea," Anne said. "Belinda is just tetchy because you left the coven and disappeared for a week with a boy. And I know Drew is a good kid. You could do a lot worse."

Everyone assumed Drew and I had hooked up. We'd shared our auras, not our bodies. I didn't even want him like that. Our connection dove deeper than the physical and had nothing to do with lust. Even if it did, I respected Claire so much more than that. She'd saved my life at least as much as I'd saved hers.

If I had feelings for someone, I had them for Claire. She stood strong in the face of danger and had never met a challenge she couldn't overcome. Except I didn't like girls. At least, I didn't think so. How did a person even know that?

Never mind. Anne kept talking.

"We could suggest something you can do to convince Belinda that you should have more autonomy."

Stace cleared her throat. "I promised tea. You might want it for this." She left the room.

I frowned, not sure what she meant. "I just want her to see me as a person instead of...a problem."

Anne sighed. "She doesn't see you as a problem. She sees you as a little girl she needs to protect. It's not that strange for a parent to have trouble accepting their child is growing up. With you, she's doubly worried because you can't defend yourself. There are plenty of dangerous things that would ignore you if you weren't magically active. Your mom is terrified you'll be targeted by something when she's not around to prevent it. I'm worried about that too. The whole coven is."

I felt my shoulders bunching as guilt pressed on me. "I left the coven."

Stace returned with a steaming wooden mug and handed it to me. "You're still family, Sophie. You didn't renounce your bloodline."

They wanted me to prove myself. If it helped, I supposed I could do some stupid task. After reminding me of all my shortcomings, they wouldn't send me out to do something so hard it would kill me.

"I guess. What do you think I should do?"

CHAPTER 6

I stepped outside and shivered in the frigid air. They wanted me to find a specific place and do a specific thing, which didn't sound hard. No one in the coven could do it because they all had too much power, or so Anne claimed. That meant I couldn't get Drew or Claire to help me, because they also had too much power.

Not that I wouldn't take Drew's help to get there. His binding to the node allowed him to use ley lines to travel in an eyeblink. When I reached the road, I found and tugged on the metaphysical cord binding us.

Sky blue streamers formed a sphere beside me. They cleared within moments, leaving Drew standing beside me. He draped a long, emerald green coat over my shoulders. The moment the thin fabric touched me, my whole body warmed. I slipped my arms into the sleeves.

Drew took my hand. Sky-blue streamers wrapped around us for half a second, then faded. We stood in a small parking lot edged by trees. I didn't recognize the spot. It could've been any of a few dozen small parks scattered across the region.

He slipped his arm around my waist and urged me to walk with him to Gabe's car. "We picked up lunch. I thought you might need something by now."

"I guess you guys have had some time to talk." The thought filled me with a kind of dread, though I couldn't explain what bothered me about it.

"A little, yeah. Mostly about coven politics. I had no idea competition over roses was that fierce. He said you're not allowed to actively sabotage each other, but everything else is on the table, and it's a huge rivalry that's been ongoing for a century. Which, I mean, I understand that people can get riled up over their passions, but this sounds kind of...excessive."

"It's about pride. Family history." I didn't want to talk about the festival, or about roses at all. "I'm not that into the whole thing. It's kind of stupid, and I don't have enough power to work on most of it. I helped keep the roses disease-free. Nothing more."

He squeezed my hand. "If you wanted to, you have access to enough power to outdo them all."

The idea of engaging with their petty little rose rivalry turned my stomach. "Ugh. No."

Drew opened the car door for me and helped me into the front passenger seat. I wanted to sit in his lap again, but I obediently climbed in and let him shut the door for me. Gabe handed me a takeout bag and a paper cup with steam rising from the tiny holes in the lid.

"Where to next?"

"Witch's Castle."

Gabe nodded and off we went.

Drew, on the other hand, asked, "What?"

I sniffed the cup and discovered hot cocoa. "Witch's Castle. It's an abandoned park ranger station and bathroom in Macleay Park." I thought everyone knew about it. Drew had grown up in foster care, though, moving from home to home, so I supposed he'd never made enough friends to hear the stories.

"Popular party hangout," Gabe said. "Friday nights are wild there."

"Everybody thinks it got its name from some stupid teenager prank or something. But it actually got its name because it has a power sink. I need to go there and climb into it." Inside the bag, I found a still-warm panini oozing with cheese. The smell made my stomach gurgle and beg.

Drew opened his mouth and shut it. "I have a question. A few questions. Most of them are of the what and why variety. Let's start with what a power sink is."

Of course he didn't know. Almost everything he knew about witchcraft had come from me, and I hadn't mentioned it. The concept had never come up because we'd never encountered one.

"It's a pool of power like a node, except not connected to ley lines. I don't know how they form or exist, I just know they do."

His lip curled. "That last part is my least favorite explanation for magical things. Not knowing how things work and using them anyway is how we get into trouble. I should know. I've done it enough. Something bad usually happens." He pointed to the tattoo of abstract roses covering the right side of his face.

"What caused that, by the way?" Gabe asked.

"The Portland node."

Gabe whistled, suggesting he understood more about nodes than I expected. "It's awake?"

Drew nodded.

We didn't need to get distracted by the past. The future could mean a happy reunion with my mom and some kind of cooperative arrangement with the Petal Society. Like Anne and Stace had said, they were still family.

"I need to dive into the sink and bring something back."

"Diving into a sink sounds simple," Drew said. "I'm guessing it's really dangerous."

"It's like diving into a node."

He frowned. "That's not dangerous for us. We both have focus stones and my binding to the node protects us from power surges. What's the catch? Is it about a thing you have to do to get there?"

I shrugged. "There's no catch. No one else can do it because they can't withstand the sink. Anne said using power to shield against the sink makes it stronger instead of weaker." That explanation didn't quite make sense to me, but I trusted Anne. "So the key is at the bottom, waiting for someone who can both survive the sink by being too weak to resist it, and also see it. Like me."

Drew sighed. "This is about the Petal Society."

"This is about my mom."

"No offense," Gabe said, "but your mom is kind of a bitch."

I wrestled with the urge to defend Mom. She wanted to protect me. Her methods hurt, but sometimes the right thing hurt. Or did it? I didn't know anymore. Why did I want to say those things? She didn't deserve my loyalty anymore.

Reaching between the seats, Drew offered his hand to me. "Can you give me one good reason why I should help you wriggle back under her thumb? Just one."

Gabe glanced at the hand. "That goes for me too."

They didn't understand. Not really. "The whole point is to prove to her that I'm not a child and don't need her protection."

Drew huffed. "You don't need to prove anything to her! She showed you who she is. Believe her. Walk away."

"You don't get it." I crossed my arms tight enough to hug myself. "If you had a mom, you'd get it."

Gabe frowned.

Drew's hand disappeared. "Sure. That's how things work." Blue light flashed in the rearview mirror, and I knew he'd left the car.

I covered my face. Why had I said that? Maybe Mom treated me like a child because I deserved it.

At least I knew Drew wouldn't shut me out for long. The next time I mustered the courage to contact him, I'd apologize. We'd talk. By then, he wouldn't feel the immediate sting anymore, and I would've figured out why I said something that cruel.

Peeking through my fingers, I checked Gabe. He watched the road. A few minutes later, the car stopped. We'd reached the park.

Awkward silence hung in the car. Gabe shut off the engine. We sat, both looking at trees through the front windshield. I opened my mouth to ask him to come with me, but couldn't muster the courage.

"Are you going to do this?"

Was I? I looked at my hands as if they had answers. "Yeah." Why? I had nothing better to do, I supposed.

But I knew the real reason. Once upon a time, my mom had watched me with fondness. She'd thought of me as her daughter instead of a witch with too little power. I remembered that smile and craved it. When I did what she wanted, she let me see a flicker of it.

I opened the car door and stepped out, protected from the cold by the coat Drew had brought for me. He thought of things like that. And I'd kicked him in the face for it.

"Do you want me to come with you?"

Did I want Gabe there? I didn't know. "If you want."

He stood and frowned at me over the car's hood. "I asked what you want. If I wasn't willing to go, I wouldn't have offered."

I shrugged. Then I met his gaze. Something in his eyes, or maybe the set of his jaw, made me think he needed someone to want him without using him for some scheme or ulterior motive. "If this wipes me out, I'll need help getting back to the car. So yeah, you coming would be great."

He nodded and locked the car. We headed into the park together.

I prayed to no one for this not to be a huge mistake.

CHAPTER 7

I wanted to ask Gabe fifty million things as our shoes squelched through the mud and damp leaves of the forested path. He didn't owe me any answers, though. Now that I knew why he'd lurked around me so much, I felt even better about leaving the coven. Neither of us had to pretend anything anymore.

Fifteen minutes from the car, the silence gnawed at me. I barely knew Gabe. Trusting him to watch my back gave me an itch between my shoulder blades. For all I knew, he'd lied to make his spying mission easier. Likewise, he had no reason to trust me about leaving the coven.

One question bothered me more than the rest. The Rose Quarter coven, like the Petal Society, had over two dozen members. At least half had kids. Though I didn't know the membership as well as I knew the Petal Society, I did know they had several sons close to my age among the kids.

"Why you?"

"Why me what?"

"Spying on the Petal Society. Why did they pick you instead of one of your cousins? Or your little brother, for that matter."

"Oh. That." Gabe sighed. "I'm not supposed to talk about it. I mean, it's not a normal thing. Can I trust you not to tell anyone?"

I opened my mouth to agree, then stopped myself. "I can't keep important things from Drew."

"Even when he's mad at you?"

Did I have anything to lose by explaining the situation to Gabe? Not really. His mom and the Rose Quarter coven didn't matter. Drew and I had no stake in their battles with the Petal Society. If the Rose Quarter decided to pre-emptively start a war with us for some reason, we had a place to withdraw that they couldn't reach, and nothing could block Drew from it.

"Drew and I accidentally merged our auras, so we have a permanent link. On top of that, we've formed our own two-person coven. He's not going to break up with me or something. We're stuck with each other forever." I shrugged. "Yeah, even when he's mad at me, or I'm mad at him, or whatever happens."

"Oh. Huh."

We walked. A gust of wind shook leafless branches and knocked powdery snow off evergreen boughs. Everything smelled like pine and rotting leaves.

"The guy my mom is married to isn't my real dad. My real dad is actually a river god." Gabe scooped a hand through the air. Several feet in front of him, streaks of white sparkled in the sun as they streamed together and collected into a wad of snow about the size of a tennis ball. "I can manipulate water in all its forms." He swatted the air, and the snowball zipped to the side.

Water foiled most kinds of magic. Drop an enchanted item, like my coat, into a river, and all the magic on it dissolved. The amount of power or effort put into its creation made no difference. Rain short of a downpour or a splashing didn't have the same effect, though it did dampen everything until it dried.

They'd sent him because he could defend himself. He could sabotage anything we did. If needed, he could disable us all.

Gabe was a weapon.

"Did she know? About your dad, I mean. Before she...you know...?" Part of me cringed in horror at the audacity of asking that gross a question.

The rest of me harbored so much curiosity that I didn't care.

"Before she seduced him?" He shrugged. "I never asked, but knowing my mom? Probably."

I shuddered at the level of cold calculation that must have taken. "Does your dad know? Her husband, I mean."

"He knows I'm not his, but he has no idea I'm god-spawn. He doesn't know anything about magic. Neither does my little brother."

My dad didn't know anything either. To me, the evidence shouted, loud and clear, that witches lived at my house. He didn't notice.

Their house. Not my house. I would never go back there, not even to visit.

Maybe to visit. Dad still cared. At least, I thought he did. He'd taken my brothers hiking even though I stayed missing, so did he? Had Mom put a compulsion on him to forget about me? Could she even do that?

"You're frowning hard enough to break something."

At his words, I noticed the usual tension in my neck and unusual tightness of my face. Relax, Sophie. Problems like this take time to solve. Magic won't help.

"Are you sure you want to do this? There's no reason you have to dive into the power sink today. It can wait."

"Once school starts tomorrow, I'll find a dozen reasons to put it off again and again. It'll never happen." I'd never gain anything like respect from my mom.

Gabe stopped and set a hand on my shoulder. "Is that bad? Your mom doesn't sound any better than mine, just different. I stay with my mom because my dad lives in the river and doesn't have an address. Plus the compulsion threats. If I left, she'd find me. But you? You've got somewhere else to go."

I met his gaze, grateful for the concern he showed. "If you had some option that might convince your mom to back off and let you live your life, wouldn't you have to try it?"

He sighed and let his arms hang at his sides. "Yes. Yes, I would." He understood. I could see it in his eyes. Drew couldn't wrap his head around this, but Gabe could. "Let's get this over with."

We continued up the path, and rounded the last turn before reaching a clearing with picnic benches. Beyond it, yellow-green moss covered the partial walls and stone roof of the Witch's Castle ruin like fur. Dried brown fern fronds decorated the footprint. Damp, rotting leaf litter clustered in piles. Soot marked the stone-ringed firepit to the side. Layers of graffiti formed unintentionally complex pictures.

Even with walls between me and it, I sensed the power sink. Feathers of bright white energy, pure and unclaimed, flickered through the window holes of the second room.

Both of us stopped at the same time.

"Can you see it?"

Gabe shook his head. "I can feel it, like when the clouds pass and the sun beats on your skin."

I reached for his hand, suddenly wanting physical reassurance and support. Deciding to do this from far away took a lot less courage than facing it.

He squeezed my hand. "If it doesn't have any feeding lines, I could try to drown it."

The power sink depleting would make my job so much easier. If it didn't backfire. "You might destroy the thing inside it."

"That would be bad, I guess." His uncertainty echoed my own. "I'll keep watch."

"Thanks."

Letting go of him took a monumental force of will. I stepped forward. My stomach churned.

Too fast, I reached the open doorway to my doom. In the center of a room with a partial roof, the glowing sphere hovered an inch above the ground. Tendrils of energy writhed across its surface like solar flares.

The power burned bright and hot like a tiny star. Drew's energy bolstered the outer edges of my aura, keeping me safe. If I stayed on the spot, nothing bad would happen.

For the past four years, everyone had told me to choose the safe route. I didn't have the ability to handle a node or a sink. They'd destroy me, one way or another. Diving into either, according to Mom, could kill me.

I hadn't come this far to give up at the threshold. Safety didn't get the job done. I needed to take a plunge, to do the stupid thing. Anne had said I'd manage fine, and I believed her. The power should ripple over me, doing nothing worse than stinging.

Besides, at this point, I didn't think I feared death so much. Dead people felt no pain. Dead people didn't have anyone trying to control them and their lives.

Dead people also didn't have friends like Drew or Claire. Or Gabe.

No, never mind that. I could do this. Anne and Stace wouldn't have sent me if they didn't believe I could handle it. Like they said, I hadn't renounced my bloodline, just the coven. Mom didn't want a burned-out witch with no power. She wanted a daughter she could be proud of.

Two steps closer, I pressed against the sink, like two balloons forced together. The tendrils groped me, searching for a weakness. I gulped and ran my hands over the sink, returning the favor.

My focus stone warmed against my chest.

Taking another step closer hurt. The power scorched and blinded me. Drew fed me, soothing my aura almost as fast as it flickered. According to Anne, it should've washed over me, and Drew's power should've made it worse, not better.

Never mind Anne and what she said. I'd work with what I found. Faster. I'd work faster to avoid as much of this situation as possible.

I focused my defenses on my fingers as they crawled over the surface, searching for imperfections while the power burned my arms. The sink didn't affect my shields. Anne had said it would steal the power I pumped into my shields and use it against me. But it didn't.

A tendril slashed across my face, breaching what shielding I could muster and leaving a jagged trail of agony in its wake. Would any of this leave scars? How would I explain them?

There! I stuck my finger into a divot and pressed with a tiny thread of power, too weak to force it to flare.

And I prayed for this not to turn into a disaster.

CHAPTER 8

I fell through white mist, which confused me. Everyone talked about big pools of magic burning them, searing their aura. Drew had described diving into the Portland node as a test of endurance against a scalding force trying to incinerate him. He'd faced a bizarre metaphysical scenario, but he'd been trying to accomplish something specific.

Since I wanted to find something, I expected the sink to flood me with power until I gave up or saw the key hiding in plain sight. Finding that imperfection should have taken me deeper into the pain or washed it over me. None of this made sense according to Anne and Stace.

My body thumped against a cloud in the fog. The impact shocked more than hurt. Rising to my hands and knees on a lumpy surface, I watched the fog recede to reveal the exact same surroundings I'd just left.

Brown and yellow moss grew from cracks and covered the top edges of graffiti-strewn partial walls and roofs. Leafless trees jabbed their barren branches into the sky. Bright sunshine threw harsh shadows on shriveled ferns and a mushy sludge of mud and dead leaves.

Had the sink rejected my intrusion, or did it want to play games? I saw no sign of Gabe, so I guessed the latter. Besides, everything tasted like paper.

If I called Drew, he'd know for sure. Except he probably wouldn't come. Unless I signaled an emergency, I expected him to ignore me for the rest of the day. Signaling an emergency when I didn't have one sounded like a great way to piss him off even more.

"I want the key," I murmured. Getting what I wanted required focusing on it and paying attention. Not knowing what it looked like or what purpose it served made focusing on it hard. I touched my chest, pressing my focus stone against my flesh.

Nothing happened. Standing and thinking probably wouldn't make the key sprout legs and find me, so I explored the ruin.

The graffiti seemed more complex than before. Letters popped out of the stones, their edges sharp enough to cut flesh. In my peripheral vision, I noticed movement from one of the weird creature paintings. When I turned to see it, the animation stopped.

I poked a glob of moss to see what would happen. Sprouts grew and expanded the colony fast enough to watch. Worried it might speed up and engulf everything, I withdrew my hand. The colony stopped growing.

Climbing to the top of a set of stairs, I avoided touching anything with bare skin. My new perch gave me a view of the whole ruin. The building didn't cover much space. Beyond it, the path stretched in two directions, flanked by barren trees. Nothing attracted my attention.

"I need a hint," I grumbled.

Wind blasted against my back so hard I fell off the stairs. More than anything, I wanted to avoid real harm. The ground yielded enough to keep me intact. Hitting it still hurt. Groaning, I rose to my hands and knees and wondered what kind of hint this place thought it gave me.

A lighter breeze stirred leaves and blew my hair into my face. Bits of dead leaf drifted in the air, floating through the archway exit.

Oh. Duh. Direction. It wanted me to go that way.

I scrambled to my hands and knees, then stood with a remarkable lack of pain to follow the flying leaf litter. Once I started down the path, the wind stopped. Seeing nothing special, I kept going. The key wasn't in the ruin. Message received.

The path carried me to an empty parking area. I licked a finger and tested the wind. Light breezes directed me up the road, past scattered houses. The forest and its overgrown retaining walls gave way to a neighborhood full of empty trees flanking houses overgrown with ivy and rhododendrons. No cars passed me. Weeds grew in cracks. Instead of blue or gray, the sky was brown. Sickly yellow clouds with black linings drifted overhead. The scent of death, of rotting carcasses, drifted in the air.

No longer able to discern the direction of the wind, I stopped in the middle of the road. The sink wanted me to see Portland abandoned for some reason.

Then I noticed the school across from my parents' house. I sprinted for the house, not sure what to expect.

Instead of a house, I found a towering dome of thorny rose canes. Yellow spots ringed with black, the mark of rose blight, peppered them. Something beyond them glowed with golden light.

Of course the key would hide inside my own house, and of course I'd have to fight my way into a place I'd fought to escape.

Never mind the emptiness around me, because I didn't know what that meant. The roses, on the other hand, I understood.

I circled the dome, looking for a weak point. All the way around, thorns gleamed in the sepia light as an impenetrable mass of pain. When I stopped and reach toward it, the thorns shifted to block the glow. Like Mom. Whatever I wanted, she always stood in the way, waiting to hurt me if I stepped out of line.

Giving up sounded good. I didn't have the tools to deal with this problem, I didn't care about the key, and I didn't need my family or the Petal Society. Drew had a point about meddling with magic I didn't understand. What could the key do? Anne had said it would prove my competence to Mom. We hadn't discussed its capabilities.

Turning my back on the dome, I sat on the curb. Dead leaves swirled in wind eddies. Empty branches creaked. Metal squeaked in the distance.

Portland was never this quiet.

"Is this supposed to be a warning? Does everybody die if I take the key? Who even put the key here?"

I rubbed my face and tried to imagine life without my dad, my brothers, my aunts, and my cousins. For one week, I'd experienced that. The best word for it? Relief. No one had treated me like a little kid or a porcelain doll. Drew thought I had a lot of value. Claire trusted me. Her family liked me. I'd helped watch Claire's two little sisters, and I'd pitched in with the cooking.

At home, I did a ton more chores, some of them for my brothers. The coven piled mundane tasks on me because I couldn't do anything else. Everyone treated me like a drudge. I'd never noticed it before I spent that week with Drew and Claire.

For some unknown reason, I wanted that life back. Familiarity, I supposed. Screw that. I didn't need to hack my way through thorns to get a key that probably did something bad.

And why had they sent me? Anne and Stace had insisted only I could do it because only I had a small enough well. But that made no sense at all. Less power meant I couldn't protect myself as well. Whatever the thorns concealed, having a pile of power wouldn't hinder. It would help.

Feeling like maybe I'd misunderstood them, I rubbed my face and thought harder about leaving.

Except...I still didn't know what the key could do. If the coven wanted it, they'd find another way to get it. I probably offered the easiest option for whatever reason. Without me, though, they just needed to try something else.

If I took the key, the coven couldn't have it. Maybe I'd still hand it over with a demand for something in return. Something more than Mom's promise not to mess in my head anymore. Portland had more than one coven, and I could demand recognition for the one I'd formed with Drew. Mom would have to stop trying to break it.

Even better, the key might offer me a direct path to real autonomy without having to hold it hostage. Maybe I could use it.

I stood and faced the thorns. Nothing came to mind for dealing with them. The coven had spent so much time telling me I couldn't do anything that I didn't know what my power could actually do. Drew and I had practiced basic, foundational stuff. We could pass power back and forth, tie enchantments to objects, and block raw power. I knew how to manipulate plants—

Hi, my name is Sophie, and I'm a moron.

Reaching with care, I poked my finger between thorns to touch a stem. The smooth, glassy surface pulsed with heat. A desire to walk away swam into my mind. I felt it creep up my arm like a shiver.

The sink wanted me to give up and go away. Everything in this place wanted me to question my purpose. Mission accomplished. I'd questioned it and decided to do it anyway.

Some of the doubt definitely came from me. The rest, I focused my will on denying. Tingling built at the base of my skull, a manifestation of the act of pouring my own power into a fight against the sink.

Most of the power I summoned came from Drew. He had so much more at his command that I looked like a drop of water compared to his Columbia River. Though he could cut me off, he wouldn't. Not without showing up to determine if I needed it to save my life.

My power shoved the sink's intrusion down to my elbow. The focus stone on my chest heated as I used it to concentrate on what I wanted. Under my assault, the sink's fingers oozed down my arm. It receded enough to let my will reach the cane I touched.

The canes around my fingertip shattered. Shards of green glass exploded in every direction. A thousand tiny razor blades sliced me. The golden glow hit me with the force of a freight train, knocking me off my feet. Intense heat burned my flesh.

It should've blasted around me. Anne had said it wouldn't hurt this much. Why had she lied to me?

Focus, Sophie. Later, when I didn't have this sink trying to kill me, I could worry about it. Claire wouldn't give up in the face of this, so I wouldn't give up.

I dragged myself into the searing pain.

CHAPTER 9

Calling Drew into this without any kind of warning could kill him. I kept moving with my head down. Lifting my chin seemed like it would melt my eyeballs, and that sounded bad. As I wriggled closer, the flesh on my fingers blistered. Every inch of my face screamed with agony. At least my jacket, as a magical construct with an enchanted aura, remained intact.

I forgot what cold felt like. Bubbles formed on my fingers. They popped. Blood inside sizzled in the air. Every breath scorched my lungs with the stench of copper and sulfur. Strands of my hair danced free of its ponytail, shriveling from the ends to my scalp.

My elbow hit the ground, I pushed with my knee, and I lurched another inch forward. I would not give up. Drew's power surged around me, protecting me from the worst of it. Without that, I wouldn't survive. With it, I stood a chance.

Another inch closer and I wondered how often witches like me happened. Everyone I knew had a deep well. They could gather power and hold it in reserve. If they stood close enough to a ley line and had a focus stone, they could draw power directly from the world and spin it according to their will. Some, like Drew and Mom, didn't even need a focus stone.

Sophie, on the other hand? I had a shallow, thin well. I couldn't draw power from a ley line and use it at the same time, even with my focus stone. One or the other for me. What little I could store barely covered ripening a flower bud.

Drew waltzing into my life had changed the game. Mom saw his aura mixed into mine, but she couldn't tell how it worked. No one could figure out how we worked by looking. They had to ask or watch us in action.

Anne had thrown me into this insane quest on purpose. If she'd known anything about the process itself, she'd sent me knowing I couldn't handle it and had lied to my face about it. Had the coven decided to get rid of me for my mom's sake? Or did they want the key so badly they'd decided to sacrifice me or my meager witch ability to get it?

If she hadn't known and thought it would only take me surviving the initial jump, I had no idea what to think of her. She always knew everything, except for this. How much of her so-called knowledge did she fake to keep me in line? I didn't even play a part in the rose competitions.

The blazing heat over my neck told me I'd reached the source. Thank goodness I didn't have to stand because I didn't think I could.

I squeezed my eyes shut and rolled onto my back. Flesh bubbles on my neck popped and oozed. My throat burned. Mustering every ounce of strength I had, I shoved my arm upward and groped in the air.

My fingers found something long and thin. Touching it burned harder than anything, ever. I felt my eyes melting. Metallic ooze dribbled through my mouth. Wrapping my hand around the thing I'd found, I willed it to obey me.

With one last burst of effort, I yanked the thing to me. My hand hit my chest and the heat died like someone had flipped a switch. I snapped open my eyes and gasped for air in the real world. Gabe rushed to my side and filled my vision. Drew did the same, crouching on the other side.

"Are you okay?" Gabe asked.

I giggled.

Drew raised his brow. "Sounds like no, and also yes. The sink is drained and your aura is a mess, so that's understandable."

As far as I could tell, none of the burning I'd experienced had carried over. My hand held a warm piece of gritty metal, but otherwise, everything had happened only in my mind. No, wait, something warm dribbled from my nose. Blood.

Each boy took one of my arms and helped me sit up.

I clutched Drew's sleeve, tugging it to make him look at me. The opportunity to apologize had jumped into my lap, and I didn't have enough stupid in me not to take it. "I'm sorry I said that. About your mom. It was mean. You don't deserve mean."

He frowned. I'd expected him to smile. "Thanks." Nothing more. He wiped my nose with a tissue.

Wind circled around Drew, stirring the dead leaves. He blinked and turned, still holding my arm. The tiny whirlwind widened until it surrounded Gabe and me also.

"What are you doing?" Gabe asked.

Drew shook his head. "It's not me."

Streamers surrounded us like Drew's did when he shifted from place to place. Instead of his sky blue, these flared white. They encased us in a loose cocoon. A heartbeat later, they dissipated, leaving us inside a dark tunnel.

Strike that. Blinding node power filled the tunnel, blazing like ten thousand suns. We sat at the base of an empty doorway to the room holding a node. If the power sink had burned like a bonfire, the node raged like a nuclear blast furnace. I couldn't even comprehend the sheer, staggering amount of pure magical power contained in the next room, pulsing in time with a heartbeat that didn't match mine.

I'd never seen a node before. In theory, I knew they could awaken into sentient beings. This one had done so, and I didn't think the coven knew about it yet. If they did, they hadn't said anything in my hearing.

Drew hopped over Gabe and me to stand between us and the node. "Get out of here," he urged.

"Are these sacrifices?" The node's voice echoed and rumbled, made of car horns honking, horses neighing, voices murmuring, women screaming, cats howling, dogs barking, crows shrieking, and concrete breaking. It sounded like a city.

"No." Drew waved his hand behind his back, shooing us. "Why have you summoned me?"

I sat on the dusty, dirty floor, transfixed and unable to move. At some point, I figured I needed to talk to Drew more about the mom thing. Later. For the moment, I couldn't stop gaping like an idiot.

Gabe didn't get up either.

We faced the Portland node. I knew because Drew had forged a soul binding with it for reasons I didn't understand. Claire had said something about saving his hide because he'd done something stupid. I believed her. He wouldn't have acted like this against any other node.

The impossibly huge wellspring of power pulsed until a partial figure bubbled to the surface. The shape refused definition except for its head. Long, fiery hair splayed around it, rippling as if it hovered underwater. The facial features seemed androgynous as far as I could tell.

The node leaned forward and peered over Drew's shoulder.

Drew shifted to block its view. "You own me, not them. What do you want from me?

Part of it formed an arm. That arm reached for my foot. I squeaked and bounced my leg like that would somehow stop it from grabbing me.

"Stop it!" Drew kicked the arm. "They aren't yours, and they don't want to be."

"That is not your decision to make," Portland said.

Five more arms snapped out of the node, reaching for both Gabe and me. One punched through my chest. Everything spun. When my stomach wanted to rebel, it stopped.

I faced my mom in my bedroom.

Abject failure crashed around me. Not only had I never mustered the courage to leave my house, but I'd also experienced something real enough to call hallucinations. She'd ripped me apart more than I'd thought, and I would never recover.

Then I noticed her hair fluttering in a breeze. Mom could do that, of course. If she wanted to, she could cause all kinds of dramatic effects. The energy involved, or so she claimed, made it too wasteful to bother.

The real giveaway? Her aura. Like normal, it flickered on the edge of my ability to perceive. Not like normal, the flickering had no blue tint. This woman had a pure white aura. Like a ley line or a power sink. Or a node.

"Portland?"

"Yes." She smiled the same way Mom did when I obeyed her without question.

"I don't want to make a deal with you."

Her brow lifted and her smile faltered. "No? Binding to me would benefit you greatly."

I covered my face. Why did she want me? No one else did. "I'm not worth your time when you already have Drew."

Feather-light caresses brushed across my arms and back. "I see you. Discounted for not having enough of a wondrous gift that transcends humanity. I chose Drew because he fell into my web. But I choose you because you're a greater witch. Knowledge, skill—these are much more valuable than raw power. Trust in yourself and no one will ever defeat you again."

The node wrapped around me, holding me in an embrace so warm and comforting that I lost track of myself. What it offered, I wanted.

No wonder Drew had let the node mark him. It accepted without judging, loved without needing, and gave without taking.

"Help me," I whimpered.

The node kissed my cheek. Blinding, glorious heat spread from its lips outward, engulfing the right side of my face.

"I sponsor your coven, not just Drew."

The warmth receded until I sat in Drew's arms. Tears streamed down my cheeks, and I didn't know why. The right side of my face stung.

"I'm sorry," Drew murmured.

Gabe sat opposite us, leaning against the wall with an empty stare. Light spilled from the right side of his face, burning a tattoo of roses across his cheek, forehead, and jaw. Like Drew.

Like me.

Portland had claimed and marked all three of us.

CHAPTER 10

Portland gazed down at us with a satisfied smile. For once, I'd done something right. I'd pleased someone more powerful than me. My new patron didn't see me as a disappointment or a waste. I reveled in her pleasure, in the pride she showed for me.

"Why did you do that?" Drew scowled. "You didn't need to bind them."

"Hush." The node reached with an impossibly long arm to touch a finger to his lips. "So much anger today. I brought you here for a reason."

Drew huffed and crossed his arms. If Gabe and I hadn't been there, I thought he would've turned his back on the node and stormed away.

"You didn't even give them a choice."

"I did." The node kissed his forehead. "They each chose for themselves. Now you have the support you need. Don't worry, you're still first among them to me."

Drew mumbled something unintelligible. Did he care that much about being special to the node? Maybe. Boys had weird ideas sometimes. The only male with witch powers I'd ever heard of needed to be more special than that for his ego or something.

"You are my coven now, my eyes and ears. My sword when needed." She brushed her fingertips down his cheek. "There is something disturbing the lines to the east. I will send you there, and you will fix it."

White bands surrounded us.

We got nothing more to work with? I raised a hand. I would've liked to ask the node about the key before she threw us into something else. "Wait!"

The white bands cleared before the sound of my voice faded. We sat in a forest of both evergreen and deciduous trees. Dead leaves and needles covered the muddy ground. Instead of the usual shrubs huddling beneath tall trees, rosebushes blanketed a wide swath of space in front of us. They covered an area at least thirty feet long and wide. I'd worked with enough of the plants to recognize the thorny, leafless canes of tea roses.

Gabe fell over. Drew and I struggled to stay sitting up without the wall behind us. I dropped the key.

The moment he regained his balance, Drew shook his head to clear it. Then he hopped to his feet and kicked a tree. He growled and swung a punch at the air. The noises streaming out of his mouth sounded like words, but he muttered so low and grumbled so much that I couldn't understand any of them. I got the gist, though. That much anger didn't need specific words.

"Are we dead?" Gabe asked, airy and disoriented.

"No." I scrambled to his side and helped him sit up. "But I don't know where we are."

Tea roses didn't grow wild in forests, not even in Portland. The shrubs showed no signs of pruning or anything eating them. Its healthy, hibernating canes stuck in odd directions and seemed integrated with the trees, like they'd grown here for many years. Each clump of canes had the same formations and thorn types, so I guessed they'd all spawned from a single plant.

Drew stopped his muttered tirade and crossed his arms. He swung his head from side to side, then stalked to his left. "I'll be back," he grumbled.

"What's wrong with him?" Gabe touched the fresh tattoo on his face.

I knew Drew well enough to at least see past the immediate, obvious answer. "He's mad at himself for putting us in the position of being bound to the node. At least, I think that's it."

"The node. Wow. I just— No words."

"Yeah." Something wholesome and pure had touched me at a moment when I'd needed it.

Gabe shook his head. "He's amazing."

"He?" I blinked at him. "The node was a woman."

"Not to me. I saw a man."

I knew Drew thought of the node as female. The implications... Maybe I felt more about Claire than I wanted to admit. Didn't people figure this stuff out before sixteen? Didn't I already have more than enough to worry about?

"Sophie?" Mom's voice made me freeze. "What are you doing out here?"

Gabe and I both turned to see Mom approaching from the opposite direction Drew had gone. She carried one of her big shopping bags slung over her shoulder. As her gaze settled on Gabe, she turned it to a glare.

"You, young man, better have a good explanation for abducting my daughter. I invited you to our house to see her, not to help her run away like a petulant child."

I blinked at her like a moron. "I, um, we...uh." A petulant child. She saw me as the one who'd done wrong. Of course she did. Why did that surprise me?

Gabe likewise failed to come up with anything brilliant to say. He ducked his head.

"At least you're exercising better judgment by running off with Gabe instead of that other boy." She adjusted the straps of her bag like she meant to set it down and open it, but changed her mind and decided to keep it hanging from her shoulder. "What happened to your face?"

Reaching up, I touched the new tattoo and winced. Gabe, I noticed, turned away from her so she wouldn't see his.

"Stop acting stupid." Mom reached us and crouched in front of me.

She took my chin in her hand and inspected me. I didn't resist. I couldn't resist. "Your aura is different. What have you done now? Did that abomination do this to you?"

"Oh, hi, Mrs. Harris," Drew said. I tried to turn my head to see him, but Mom wouldn't let me. "This is a weird place to run into you."

Get a grip, Sophie. Drew vs. Mom couldn't end well.

Mom shifted her glare to Drew. The amount of extra venom she summoned to direct at him stunned me. "And here he is." Poison clung to her words. "I'd say you've come to claim responsibility, but I don't think you know how."

Thinking Mom might try to take it, I covered the key with my hand. Keeping my movements slow would keep her from noticing. I focused on the goal of hiding it behind my back.

"That's rich, coming from you." Drew smirked. He seemed so calm and collected, like nothing Mom could do would ever bother him. "Maybe if you didn't treat her like a child, she wouldn't run to me. Or, you know, violate her."

Mom gasped with indignation. "How dare you? Did you get her tangled up with whatever gang you're in?" She waved at the right side of her face.

She didn't know about Drew and the node, which meant she had no basis to understand what had happened to me. Thank goodness.

Drew snorted. "Why are you out here? Did you murder Mark Terdan?"

Mom recoiled like he'd slapped her. I didn't know anything about how Claire's father had died, so I didn't know what to think. From her reaction, Mom did know a thing or two about it.

"Don't you talk about Mark!" Mom launched an attack.

I'd never seen her do that. She summoned power and flung it raw like she'd done it a thousand times.

Everyone in the coven told me magic couldn't do things like that. I'd since discovered that was wrong, but I'd never suspected they'd lied to my face. Whenever I encountered magic that didn't fit their rules, I'd assumed they didn't know it could do that.

At this point, I should've known better. Mom had done enough this morning alone to prove she didn't trust me and didn't think I could handle making decisions for myself.

I wanted to hurt her as much as she'd hurt me. No, I wanted to hurt her more. She needed to see her little toy making a choice she didn't like.

With one incredibly stupid goal motivating me, I surged to my feet and leaped into the way of her attack.

Drew shouted my name.

Gabe grunted in surprise.

Mom screamed, "Jenny!"

Raw, primal power hit my chest. Blue streamers surrounded me.

The blue cleared with me lying on a concrete slab. Wooden beams and brick walls supported the slate gray ceiling overhead. Copper pipes and silver ductwork hung from the ceiling. As I sat up, I noticed a row of bins and shelves holding roots like potatoes and garlic, jars of jam or pickled vegetables, and blocks of cheese. Chunks of meat hung from hooks, as did several branches of herbs. A specialized shelving unit held unlabeled bottles of wine on their sides.

Had Mom killed me with that blast? No, she couldn't have. My passive defenses, bolstered by Drew's power...had nowhere near enough integrity to deflect a full-force attack by someone as powerful as my mom.

I died and went to a basement. Which probably meant Hell.

CHAPTER 11

The basement didn't have an exit. My personal hell included parsnips? Also, I still held the key. I still wore the green coat and all the rest of my clothes. Touching my face revealed I still had tender skin where the node had tattooed me.

If I hadn't died, what had happened?

Mom had blasted power at Drew. I'd gotten in the way. Poof, I shifted to a metaphysical realm. Magic made no sense sometimes.

Lifting the iron key, I considered maybe the power had hit it first. What did I know about actual magical objects? Not much. I knew how to take a mundane object and enchant it so it did something specific, like cut magic or repel cold. Mom's power might have somehow activated the key. My chest still hurt, so maybe she'd blasted with more than the key needed, and the rest hit me.

Escaping the basement probably—hopefully—involved using the key. If it didn't, I had no other ideas.

First, I needed to find a lock. I touched everything in the room. The potatoes felt and smelled like potatoes, as did all the other food. I opened one of the jars. Though I knew better than to taste test random magical things, I didn't see many other options. Dipping my finger into the red goo, I pulled out a gob and stuck it in my mouth. Jam. My great-grandmother had made strawberry jam with this exact ratio of sweet and tart. She'd used fresh berries from her own garden, which had once been her grandmother's garden.

My grandma still lived in that house, and it had a cellar like this one. Mom wanted it. Gramma hadn't lost much of her steam yet, and we expected her to keep going for several more years. I harbored a secret hope she might give the house to me instead of Mom.

Strawberry jam wouldn't help me escape. Trying to replace the lid, I fumbled and dropped the jar. The glass smashed and jam splattered everywhere, including on me. Spots on my coat flickered and sizzled, then steamed. Enchantments on the coat made it self-cleaning, which didn't help my jeans or shoes.

I didn't know how to clean jam with magic and didn't want to waste my time doing it. Shaking my foot helped, but I gave up on the idea of getting rid of it all.

The bins and shelves covered sections of the walls and floor, so I tried moving them. They proved as heavy as expected. By using my legs more than my arms, I shoved three bins out of place before finding a big iron lock in the floor to match my big iron key. Sweating and panting, I stuck the key into the lock and turned.

Green light formed a glowing outline for a door. The rectangle of concrete sank into the slab, then fell open. Through it, I saw nothing but glowing green.

No matter how little I liked the idea of stepping into the unknown, I hadn't suffered through getting that key for nothing. Ducking out of this meant nothing changed. Returning to the real world meant Mom trying to break me again.

I jumped into the glow feet-first. For a long moment, the green blinded me. Peppermint like Gramma always offered when we visited threatened to overwhelm me. Wind battered me as if I fell a long distance.

Then I landed on my feet with a jarring thump, and the light dimmed to that of pleasant sunshine.

Young sycamores lined a packed-earth road. I stood in the middle of it with a canopy of leaves overhead. Sunshine filtered through the trees to create tiny, odd-shaped shadows all around me. That one looked like a wedge of cheese. Another reminded me of a butterfly. I also saw cats, roses, crescent moons, grandfather clocks, flames, and more.

Beyond the trees, mist partially obscured wooden sidewalks and building facades. The rooflines and blank signs in the fog reminded me of pictures of Portland from the early 1900s. That one could've been a general store, and this one had a sign shaped like a hand saw. I had ancestors who'd worked as carpenters.

Growling and rustling attracted my attention. Behind me, in the distance, something vague and dark moved toward me. I stared and blinked, not sure what I saw. This metaphysical realm apparently came with a guardian of some sort.

As it closed the distance, details filled in. Dozens of long, thin arms stretched in every direction. Multiple short, spindly legs twisted and writhed to propel it. The first hint of green revealed leaves on its arms. I recognized the shape.

A rosebush in the blush of late spring approached me, propelling itself by its roots.

The key had brought me to a metaphysical space, so this didn't surprise me as much as it could have. Anything could exist in a realm made of magic. Usually, it all had metaphorical anchors, but that didn't mean any of it would make sense to me.

Breezes laden with rose musk tickled the trees, shifting the leaves and dappled shadows across the road. Through the mist, I made out a sign for a post office. Why a post office? Did this have something to do with a mailman? Did I need to find something in a mailbox? This street didn't have any mailboxes in sight.

The shrubbery gained speed, charging toward me with no sign of stopping.

Faced with the possibility its thorns could rip me apart, I turned and ran for my life. People could die in metaphysical spaces. Dying in one meant dying for real. Even if my physical body hadn't crossed into this realm, and I had no way to tell, assaults on my mind would result in injury to my person. The mind translated a metaphysical blow to brain injury.

My shoes tapped on the packed earth as I sprinted, raising tiny clouds of dust and spitting daubs of mud at the same time. Did that mean I needed to use two kinds of magic to defeat the rosebush? Or did the rosebush use two types of magic? Could I escape it with something that combined dry and wet?

It roared with a great shaking of canes.

Panic kept my feet moving. I glanced over my shoulder and wished I hadn't. The rosebush continued to close the distance. Flowers bloomed as it moved, each the deep red of spilled blood. No one had ever taught me how to attack with magic. Even if I had a physical weapon, I didn't know how to use one.

From watching Mom for a split-second, I knew throwing an attack meant unleashing a lot of power. How to shape it, though, eluded me. Power couldn't just go. It had to go in a form, to fulfill a purpose. I knew it as a force for nurturing and growing, not destruction. Attacking with it felt wrong in every fiber of my being.

Rustling leaves sounded close.

At least I knew how to run. Aerobics gave me good endurance for this one thing. Moving heavy things took a lot out of me, but I could run forever. So long as I kept ahead of this thing, I didn't have a problem. This place had to have somewhere I could duck to the side or jump through a door, or something.

To my left, I noticed a dark doorway framed by a pair of sickly yellow birch trees. Their branches twined to create an archway. Film of some sort, like thick cobwebs, clung to the trees. Nothing about that path enticed me. There had to be something else.

Something swatted my leg.

I didn't stumble. More speed. I needed more speed. Rushing panic, surging through my veins, made me run faster. My knees jerked higher and my toes pushed harder against the ground. This would work. It wouldn't catch me.

Belief could sustain me in a metaphysical realm. If I knew, deep down in my heart, that I could run faster than the rosebush, then I could. These places worked that way. Whoever wanted something more, with more force and fierceness, got what they wanted. No way could this rosebush want to hurt me more than I wanted not to get hurt. Survival ranked as my top priority at all times.

Sharp pain sliced across my back.

I stumbled and screamed. Thorns ripped the flesh across my ankle. I lost my balance. The rosebush pounced. Canes whipped me, scoring lines of agony across my face, my arms, my legs. Flowers punched my eyes. Another flower shoved itself into my mouth.

Choking and gagging, I flailed my arms and legs to make it stop. The cane dove deeper. I couldn't breathe. Rose musk smothered me. Thorns slashed my hands, my clothes, my arms, my legs, my everything.

Something inside me snapped with a deafening crack like too-close thunder. I died.

CHAPTER 12

The pain shifted from my body to my head. I couldn't move. My face pressed against something warm and fleshy. Another warm thing rubbed gentle circles on my back. A thousand ants wriggled on a spot over my breastbone, giving me a weird itch I couldn't scratch.

"Come on, Sophie," Drew murmured, "climb out before it kills you."

I tried to tell him I was okay. Instead, my mouth made a mumbly, groaning sort of noise. My head hurt so much I wanted to cry again. Whoever had decided to scrape broken glass across my brain could stop anytime.

Oh, wait. That was me.

"She's awake," Gabe said.

Drew sighed. His whole body heaved with relief. He stopped rubbing my back to cradle my head and lower my body. I lay across his lap in the backseat of Gabe's car. Blood smeared Drew's neck, cheek, glasses, and jacket.

The blood attracted my attention.

"You're bleeding from your eyes, ears, nose, and mouth." Drew swiped an already bloody hand towel across my face. "I tried to join you, but it didn't work. So I pulled you out. Only that didn't exactly work either. What happened?"

My mouth still refused to work properly. Instead of words, I spewed unintelligible noises.

"Okay, don't push yourself too hard. Can you let go of the key?"

The key? I couldn't feel my fingers. Trying to make them open didn't work. My head hurt too much.

"Maybe we should take her to the hospital," Gabe said. "That's a lot of blood, and I think the shaking is a sign of shock."

Nurses at a hospital would hear my age and want to call my mom. "No!" At least I could get that word out of me.

Drew wiped more blood off my face. "Two guys bring a bleeding, underage girl to the ER. Yeah, that's gonna go well. We can see if the node will fix it? She kind of caused this, and we can't do what she wants until you're better."

He sounded like he wanted me to decide. Did we have some other option? Since he didn't suggest the obvious option of going home, I expected he had a reason. My head hurt too much to figure it out. So I trusted him.

I nodded.

"Do you want to come along?" Drew asked Gabe.

"If the node expects me to be part of all this, I probably should."

"Find somewhere to park the car, then. I'll take us to her."

Several long, agonizing minutes later, Gabe shut off the car. Drew shifted us to the node's tunnel. He buckled under my weight, which made me feel so much better about everything, especially my hips and thighs. Without a word, Gabe lifted me off the ground like I weighed nothing and carried me to the node. Drew scrambled to his feet and hurried to catch up.

We reached the room a few minutes later. I couldn't look at the node. All that power rubbed against me like sandpaper on my skin.

"Why are you here? The situation with the lines is not resolved." The node's voice stabbed me in the head.

"That's your fault," Drew snapped. "You can't just send us someplace whenever you want and expect results. We need information and time to plan. Besides, we looked and didn't see anything, and now Sophie's hurt. What can you do about that?"

The node's power retreated enough that I noticed. "I cannot repair a human body.”

"Then she'll die and it'll be your fault."

"Your anger is not helpful."

Blue streamers surrounded us. They cleared to reveal a fenced yard for a small, one-story house lined with raised garden beds. A large glass greenhouse filled most of the center.

"Where are we?" Gabe asked.

"Grandma Gert's house." Drew waved for Gabe to follow him as he headed for the back door.

Drew didn't have a Grandma Gert. I knew that because we'd researched his lineage to figure out how he and I were related. Five generations back, we had a common ancestor.

Gabe kept up with Drew, doing a great job of not jostling me. "Is she a witch?"

"No. She's an ordinary, normal person with no ties to a coven who likes baking cookies and won't call the police or an ambulance if we ask her not to."

"Are you sure she has no ties to a coven?"

"No." Drew knocked on the back door. "This is the only place I ever had the foster mom tell me I could come any time I needed help, day or night. I've never taken her up on that because I've never had a problem I thought she could help with at a time when I could get here. If she has a witch's aura, we'll leave and find someplace else."

I forced myself to cough up a single word. "Claire?"

Drew shook his head. "She can't help. Besides, no offense to you, Gabe, but I don't know you well enough to take you there. If it was just Claire, maybe that wouldn't matter, but it's our family there."

"How is Grandma Gert going to help?" Gabe practically read my mind.

"She's going to give us a safe space where we can try stuff."

The door opened. A stocky woman in a floral print dress and fuzzy pink slippers, her gray hair held up in a bun, raised her thick, gray brows at us.

"Drew!" She smiled, then she frowned. "You're covered in blood. My goodness, you're all a sight. Come out of the cold." The woman's marbled voice had a slight accent I couldn't place. French, maybe, or German. She stood aside and waved us in.

"Thanks, Grandma Gert. We just need a place to rest for a little bit." Drew kissed her on the cheek and led Gabe into the house. The floor creaked under their weight. Pictures of kids hung on the beige walls. From the fashion choices and sharpness of the photos, they ranged from the 1970s to the present.

I smelled fresh bread and chicken soup. Frank Sinatra's voice, tinny and crackling, crooned from a room we passed in the hallway.

"And to clean up, I expect. Use the back bedroom, dear. I'm not fond of that quilt. I'll be there in a minute to help."

Drew opened a dark wooden door. Gabe stepped into a small room with a queen bed and laid me on it. All the furniture and the floor matched the door. Peppermint hung in the air.

"Wake up," Grandma Gert said. She rubbed my face with a warm, damp towel.

Had I fallen asleep? My eyelids seemed so heavy. Lead weighed me down.

"Drew, this girl needs medical attention. She's lost a lot of blood. And look at her eyes. I saw plenty in my day, but I've never seen eyes like that."

"I know, but her mom will find her if we go to a doctor."

Someone picked up my hand and squeezed it.

"I have a wild idea," Gabe said.

Why couldn't I see Gabe? Why couldn't I turn my head? Everything took too much effort. I wanted to sleep.

"No, don't close your eyes, child. Stay awake." Grandma Gert swiped her warm towel over my forehead.

"Never mind the explanation," Drew said. "Try it. I'll do what I can to help."

I felt heavy. Like I clung to an anchor as it sank to the bottom of the ocean.

"Sophie." Gabe held me in his arms.

We floated underwater. I didn't enjoy swimming. Mom and the other witches hated it. Where I felt the water pressing on me, leeching away my strength, they described it as a monster sucking out their souls. This didn't remind me of swimming, though.

Drew slipped his arms around me from behind. His embrace felt like home. "You were right. This is wild."

"Focus," Gabe chided.

This reminded me of lying in a bed with Claire and Drew, a gentle green glow keeping the darkness at bay. They welcomed me when they could have cast me aside. My presence kept them from anything more than a quick, chaste kiss. Neither complained. Neither suggested turning me out so they could have privacy. Neither gave me the slightest feeling of annoyance.

Without me, they could love each other unfettered. With me, they restrained themselves. I stood in their way.

Shadows crept toward us as tendrils. They slipped around Gabe and Drew, in corkscrews, leaving darkness in their wake. Warmth fled, stealing my breath.

"What's wrong?" Drew asked. "This is making things worse."

"She has to want to live," Gabe said. "I don't think I can reach her like you can. We barely know each other."

Drew kissed my neck. "Sophie, I need you."

"No, you don't." Did I really think that? The node wanted me. Or did it really? Had Portland said what she needed to say to get me to agree? Mom did that. Maybe everyone did that.

"Yes, I do."

"You have Claire."

"Because I have a torch, I can't also want a flashlight? You're part of me, Sophie. When no one else would or could, you helped me. You saved my life and you did it in a way no one else could have. I'm not here because I feel like I need to return the favor, though. I'm here because without you in it, my life will be darker."

He lied. No, he didn't. Did he? How would I know? I couldn't tell the truth from lies anymore. My mom and the rest of the coven had lied to me for years. Until I met Drew, I'd never noticed or figured it out.

Had Ashley lied to me? Had she humored me all this time, pretending to like me despite my pathetic power well?

"Sophie, please. You matter to me."

He said that like he meant it. Most boys demanded my body. They didn't want my heart. Why would they want that? They didn't care what I wanted, either. Why would that matter?

"I'm terrible to you," I blurted.

"I've had terrible done to me. You're not even in the same ZIP code as terrible." Drew turned my head and kissed me. Unlike every other boy I'd ever kissed, his hands didn't wander. He held me close and kept me warm.

"I love you, Sophie."

CHAPTER 13

I opened my eyes in that small bedroom. Drew leaned over me, stroking my cheek with his thumb. He smiled and kissed my nose. His soaking wet hair clung to his face, and he didn't have his glasses.

"Thank you," he murmured.

"For what?"

"Choosing to live instead of die. Teaching us how to heal someone. Being yourself. Letting me in."

My eyes burned. "What about Claire?"

He grinned. "Claire is my torch, and you're my flashlight." He touched the tip of his nose to mine. "Don't worry about it. We'll all talk everything out. But not right now. Later. Right now, Gabe and I want to know what happened to you."

I was his flashlight. Did he mean that like it sounded? The links between us had brought us together by accident, and now he wanted me to find a path for him. How could I light up his darkness when I couldn't light my own?

Why did Drew love me? Why would anybody love me? Why didn't Claire come to rescue me and tell me she loved me instead of Drew? I wanted to crawl under the bed and curl up in shame that I couldn't save myself. Claire could save herself. She always did. Sophie, on the other hand? If boys didn't come for me, I'd sink to the bottom of a lake.

Drew sat up and put on his glasses with no sign he could read me. Gabe channeled the remaining water out of the bed in a stream bending out the door.

All my pain had faded to a whisper, and strength flowed through my limbs. I sat up without help. The spot on my chest still wriggled, though.

Under it, I still wanted to die. Drew didn't mean those things. He couldn't. Maybe he thought he did.

Or maybe I just had no idea what love was.

I sighed and decided I didn't know much of anything at all. "What did you do?"

"It was Gabe's idea." Drew pointed over his shoulder with his thumb. "Thanks to the node tying us all together, he and I were able to use you as a channel to merge my power with his. Our power mingled in you and brought us together."

"That doesn't make any sense." The words tumbled out of my mouth as an automatic, unthinking reaction. They sounded stupid out loud. "Except that everything I know about how magic works is a lie, so I guess it doesn't matter if I think it makes sense or not."

"Portland tied me into the coven." Gabe shrugged. "Which doesn't really make sense to me. I'm not a witch. How can I be part of a coven? Through the will of an awakened node, apparently."

"That's clearly something we'll have to explore." Drew settled on the edge of the bed and left plenty of room for me to join him.

He wanted me to sit with him. I scooted close because he expected it. The moment my arm touched his, all those dizzying questions receded. They didn't disappear, they became lesser. All my confusion and worry took a step back.

"But right now," Drew continued, oblivious to me, "we need to figure out what's going on. We found your mom in the place the node sent us to discover what's messing with local ley lines, so it seems safe to say she's at least one of the people behind it. What did she do to you?"

"I think she activated the key." I told them what happened. It didn't take long.

"Killed by a rampaging rosebush is either the best or worst imaginable epitaph." Gabe leaned against the wall in front of us with his arms crossed over his chest.

I couldn't decide if I found that funny or not.

Drew smirked. "Sounds like you'd be fine if you had some help in there." He wrapped his fingers around my wrist and raised my hand.

The key remained stuck in my grip. I couldn't even feel it against my skin, like it had become part of me.

"Don't panic." Drew patted my hand.

My face must've given me away.

He kissed my cheek. "If there's one thing I've learned, it's that panic isn't very useful around magic."

"Drew is a smart young man," Grandma Gert called from the other room. "Listen to him."

"She saw all of this?" I blinked at him. Everyone in the coven had drilled into me that we don't use magic in front of mundanes. My questioning of that had earned me lessons about the Inquisition, the Salem Witch Trials, and other moments in history like them. Sure, people had seen dragons and other magical creatures on TV last week, but they hadn't seen people or people-shaped things wielding magic.

"You wouldn't believe the things I've seen in my lifetime, girl."

Whatever that meant.

"She's not magical," Drew said. "I checked. The house is safe too."

Gabe cleared his throat. "It sounds like someone has to activate the key with a blast of raw power. Do either of you know how to do that?"

Drew nodded. "I can do that, yeah. Which means we need a way to get you into it with Sophie. Since it doesn't take you bodily there, we can stay here while we do it."

Grandma Gert stepped into the doorway holding a tray. "Would any of you like a chocolate chip cookie or three? I understand this using magic business makes you hungry."

My belly chose that moment to growl with the force of a tornado. Gabe swiped cookies and handed two to me. Drew got his own. I stuffed a cookie into my face.

"In my experience, when it comes to magic things, touch helps." Grandma Gert flashed a bright smile and left her tray in Gabe's hands.

"It might work if I'm touching the key," Gabe said.

Drew nodded. "We should probably also link auras with you before doing this. The node already tied us together, so taking it one step further may be our best option for all of us generally. And if Sophie winds up alone again," he looked to me, "you'll have more options. Hopefully."

Hope hadn't worked well for me so far, but we didn't have much choice. The node wouldn't let us walk away from everything. Mom wanted the key, and she had some involvement in the node's issues, so it had a connection. Before I faced her again, I needed to know what that metaphysical realm meant to her and why it had a key.

Someone had gone to a fair amount of trouble to hide that key.

"I don't think that power sink was naturally occurring."

Both boys stared at me.

I blushed. "I mean, it had a key inside it. The key doesn't bleed power, so it didn't make the sink. I didn't see anything else nearby that could've made it. No ley lines ran close, and nothing appeared burned out. So...I guess...I think someone built the power sink to hide the key?"

"People don't hide things for no reason," Gabe said. "Like, my mom has this collection of old keys, not a lot different from that one. She keeps them in a box. That box is in her bedroom, under the bed, inside a bigger box full of silk scarves. She keeps them there because at least one is a safeguard against something. The rest are to confuse anyone looking for it."

This time, I joined Drew in staring at Gabe.

"Why do you even know that?" Drew asked.

Gabe grinned. "When I was eight, I went searching for my Christmas presents and found that box. I thought old-fashioned keys were a weird thing to keep like that, so I, being dumb, took the ring of keys to her and asked about them."

I glanced at Drew. He met my gaze. If he didn't have the same idea as me, I'd eat my coat. "Do you think it's kind of a weird coincidence that your mom has a key a lot like this one, and the one my mom wants?"

"There's no such thing as coincidence where magic is involved," Drew said. "Do you think you could get that key?"

Grimacing, Gabe shook his head. "I doubt it. This is my parents' bedroom we're talking about. And the keys might not even be there anymore. If they aren't, I wouldn't know where else to look. Mom works from home these days, so finding time to do anything without her around is hard."

I didn't want to go anywhere near a Rose Quarter witch if I could help it. Especially not with this thing buzzing on my chest. "Let's worry about that later. Maybe one of us will have an idea while we're handling the million other things we need to work on. Besides, we know we don't need that second key to get into that metaphysical space."

"Good point." Drew offered one of his hands to me and the other to Gabe. "Let's link Gabe into our aura merge and try using the key again."

Oh, sure, we just give him a magical hug and boom, everything works. "I have no idea how to merge auras on purpose. I mean, I don't mind doing it because we're all stuck together through the node, but ours happened by accident, and you almost died. Let's not do that to Gabe." I took Drew's hand anyway because I didn't have a reason not to.

"I'm all for Gabe not almost dying. Also not actually dying." Gabe took Drew's hand. He put his other hand on my arm so he didn't touch the key still stuck in my hand.

"I'm on board for that too." Drew squeezed my hand. "We're going to try stuff. Since we don't know exactly what we're doing, and we're not sure how any of this works, it might take some time. But we've done it before, so we can do it again."

He sounded so hopeful and certain. Claire always did too. I wanted to feel that way. Just once, I wanted to face a challenge and believe in my heart that I could handle it with no doubts or questions.

Maybe someday.

Probably not.

CHAPTER 14

Drew's already potent well of power surged. I felt it like an engine against my skin revving to full speed. He'd connected to a ley line I hadn't noticed. Taking a look around, I didn't see it. To figure out where he'd tapped, I focused until I saw the silvery blue line running from him into the ground. Even then, I couldn't find the line.

The node hadn't given me much of a boost.

Why had it bothered to bind me? Knowledge, allegedly, but what did that mean? Almost everything I knew was wrong or incomplete.

"You're not useless," Drew whispered, like he could read my thoughts.

"What should I do then?" Maybe I snapped at him more harshly than I meant to.

"I'm just a battery, remember? You're the guide."

He expected me to figure this out? "You guys healed me, and I have no idea how you did that! I never would've imagined it could happen! What do you think I'm going to do? Snap my fingers and make it work because I said so? Maybe that works for Claire, but not for me. Nothing works for me."

Drew interrupted me by touching the back of my own hand to my lips. I'd yelled at him, and he smiled at me. "You got the key out of the sink. You escaped your mom. You're a survivor. Don't try to tell me you can't do anything because you can't do everything. And things don't work for Claire because she snaps her fingers. Things work for Claire because she does whatever it takes, for however long it takes, without giving up."

Gabe squeezed my hand. "I know what it's like. My mom sees me as a weapon or a tool, not a person. I'm something she can keep in a box until there's a good situation to deploy me. Every time I try to do something for myself, she hauls out the compulsion threat and the family guilt. I hate her for it, but I can't stop her on my own. I know this is about you and your mom, but it's also about me and my mom. I need this too."

I wanted to run and hide, to cry, to fling myself off a cliff, to do anything that would make the tidal wave of feelings stop crushing me.

If I had Mom at my mercy, what would I do? Part of me wanted to rip her mind to shreds like she'd done to mine. The rest of me recoiled from that dark impulse. She still loved me and wanted me. I still owed her...what? Obedience? Unconditional, unquestioning love?

How many times did I have to let her hurt me?

Hadn't she done enough?

Yes. Yes, she had. No more. It stopped today. She didn't deserve anything else from me. I'd given my pound of flesh and pint of blood. Mom wanted a little doll to dress up and marry off so I'd make more witches for her to control. Screw that.

With that decision, tension I'd built up over years seemed to ease.

I sniffled and breathed a few times. Drew kissed my cheek. Gabe squeezed my hand again.

"Okay."

With a whisper of thought, Drew's aura and mine meshed into a silver-streaked, sky blue whole. His power washed over me, like stepping into a sauna. Thick, rich, deep blue rippled around Gabe. Which made no sense. Mom would've seen that aura at a glance, but she thought he had nothing more than the common potential of a boy with witches in his ancestry.

I lifted Gabe's hand and examined his aura. Tiny flickers of green pulsed through it. The phenomenon meant nothing to me, but I thought about everything he'd told us. One conclusion made sense to me.

"Your mom screened your aura to hide it from my mom so she wouldn't figure out anything about you. But I can see it because…because the node's binding overrides it for us? That's the only thing that changed."

"Huh." Drew peered at him. "I thought you could suppress it or something, then stopped bothering in front of us after that binding."

"I can't do anything like that." Gabe frowned. "I can't see auras at all. She must've done it when she claimed she was protecting me. I guess, in a way, she was."

His mom had no moral high ground compared to mine. They both deserved some kind of a slap to the face or something. "Do you want me to remove it? I don't know if I can, but I'll try if you want."

After a moment of thought, Gabe nodded. "Yes. Whatever she's done, undo it. I don't care if it's helpful or not. She did it without explaining or asking."

I could relate to that.

"Did it hurt when she did that?" I didn't know why I asked.

"No."

Somehow, that answer bothered me. Shouldn't something like that hurt? Every time my mom had violated my trust, it had happened with pain.

Never mind. Lack of trauma didn't discount Gabe's anger. I watched his aura, trying to figure out how to access the flickering.

"You know," Gabe said, breaking my concentration, "come to think of it, that was when my nightmares started. Since right around when she did that, I've had nightmares about drowning. At first, I had them every night, and they were intense. I'd wake up gagging on water my power had summoned. Over time, they faded, though I still get them once in a while." He paused for a moment before adding, "I can't drown. Literally can't. I can breathe water. There is no chance I will ever drown. I've known that since I was five. Which makes those nightmares all the more surreal and weird."

"Maybe this will make them stop." I wished I had something so concrete to make things better for me. "Okay, guys. Be my sounding board. Whatever is wrong with his aura, it's manifesting as flickers. When Drew and I merged auras, it happened because Drew's had been sliced into a zillion pieces and mine rushed in to plug them. We obviously don't want to do that to Gabe because it hurts and could maybe kill you instead."

"If there's any question about it, I'm still for me not dying."

Drew chuckled. I smiled at Gabe.

I hovered my finger over his aura, then poked when I saw a flicker. It tasted metallic and painful. With me touching it, the flicker didn't fade. A thread connected it to another flicker.

"It's like barbed wire, only moving." I raised my head and met Gabe's gaze. "This is probably going to hurt. A lot."

He gulped. "You're going to yank it out?"

"That's my best guess. And it'll leave behind holes Drew and I can fill."

"Okay. I can take some pain."

"Go slow," Drew said.

I nodded. Yes, prolong the pain to avoid killing him. Ugh. No, don't think about that.

Removing magical barbed wire from his aura needed a metaphorical approach, like anything else. I removed my finger and tried to think of how to get rid of barbed wire. What opposed that? Something that harmed metal.

Rust, of course.

Using Drew's power, I sheathed my hand in rust. Flakes of orange and brown hovered, creating a writhing gauntlet. I held my finger over Gabe's aura again and jabbed when I saw a flicker in the right spot.

Gabe grunted in surprise.

Good. That meant I'd done something right.

I hooked my fingers around the thread attached to the flicker. Before tugging on it, I positioned my other hand to plug whatever hole I left behind. Then I pulled.

The thin cable ripped out a chunk of watery flesh. Gabe groaned. I stuck my finger into the ragged hole and shoved in power. The hole filled and healed. Gabe hissed with relief.

"Are you done already?"

"No." Instead of letting him breathe for long, I ripped out another barb and backfilled it. Judging by the distance between them and the number of flickers, I had a feeling this would take a long time. "Maybe get him something to bite down on."

"How about a toothbrush?" Grandma Gert asked.

I didn't look up from my work. The wire stretched in both directions, and if I didn't keep track of it, the barbs would touch his aura and sink in again. If I unraveled any of it, I'd have to manage two ends plus the backfilling with only two hands.

Wait. Drew could let go of me and let me use one of his hands.

I showed him how to backfill. We worked well together. Through Gabe's screams.

CHAPTER 15

Grandma Gert fed us chicken noodle soup and thick slices of toasted bread covered with half-melted cheddar cheese. We sat around her wooden dining room table, trying not to slurp as we devoured the meal with wild abandon. By the time we'd finished with Gabe, those cookies had evaporated from my belly, and I'd thought I might die without food.

"I just can't believe how much better I feel." Other than his voice, which made him sound like a longtime chain-smoker, he'd recovered completely. "It's like I was walking around under a cloud, and then the sky cleared. Everything seems brighter and...like morning dew when the sunrise hits it."

I kind of understood. Leaving the Petal Society had lifted a burden from me. Deciding not to do anything for my mom anymore had done the same. No one had covered me in barbed wire, though. None of it had restrained me magically.

"As soon as we're ready," Drew said, "we should deal with that rose monster."

"Why don't we go home to do that?" We had a safe place there to do whatever we needed, and backup on standby. Going there seemed obvious now that we'd brought Gabe fully into the coven. We could trust him.

Drew swiped a slice of cheese-covered bread through the remains of his soup and frowned into the bowl. "I'm worried about that key. Until we can pry it out of your hand and leave it someplace, I don't think I should take you there. We just don't know enough about it or why your mom wants it."

My key hand lay in my lap. I sighed and stared at it. "So I'm banished for now?"

"No, I just— We all promised not to bring anything dangerous there. I think that key qualifies as dangerous because we don't know it isn't. Yeah, it takes you on a metaphysical ride, but it also won't let you put it down."

I sighed again. He was right. Besides Claire and a few other magically active people, home had two innocent, defenseless little girls and their nonmagical mother and grandparents. Exposing them to random stuff wouldn't end well. "I'm sorry."

"It's okay." Gabe patted my shoulder.

The contact satisfied a craving I hadn't noticed until that moment. I wanted to touch him. Drew leaned toward him too, like a weak magnet.

Great. We all wanted to bask in the feel of each other. Awkward.

Gabe stuffed his last piece of bread into his mouth and picked up his water glass. He gestured to the back bedroom and raised his brow.

"Yeah, let's get to it." Drew followed Gabe's example.

"I'll just be another minute." I finished my soup while the boys headed down the hallway. Eating one-handed had slowed me down compared to them.

Grandma Gert picked up Gabe's bowl and spoon. "World War Two happened when I was a teenager. I was thirteen when it started. The Nazis overran my town in the northeast part of France early in the war. We didn't have weapons or training. Many were killed, mostly the men. It was a terrible thing.

"I tell you this because my mother decided to serve the Nazis to save me and my father. She fingered Jews for them, she told them who had valuables on their property, and she gave them the name of every young man who'd gone into the French military or run off to join the resistance. She even told them who had been knitting gloves and scarves for our military."

This story didn't sound like my problems, but Grandma Gert hadn't heard enough to know that. Partly because I had bread to eat, partly because I respected elders, and partly because a few of my ancestors had served in that war, I said nothing and let her speak.

"One day in the middle of the war, when it looked like Hitler would win, a small team of French Resistance fighters came to our town. One of their women had suffered an injury in their last battle, and they needed a place to rest and recover for a few days. A kind old lady who used to bake cookies for all the kids in our neighborhood opened her home to them.

"My mother ran to the Nazis and told them. The Nazis came and tried to burn down the lady's house. They didn't succeed because the fighters all had supernatural powers. One was a vampire. One had a very smart bird who rode on his shoulder. They killed all the Nazis and helped the lady fix what damage had been done."

A vampire had fought with the French Resistance. Sure. Why not, right?

As for the story, though, I had a feeling I knew what came next. "What did your mom do?"

Grandma Gert sighed. "We all clustered around the house as the fighters laid out the bodies. One made a speech about Vichy traitors, which is what they called Frenchmen who sided with the Germans. I remember looking at those dead men and feeling responsible. My own mother had been one of many who helped prolong the war. Nazis had carried away my friends because of my mother.

"I pointed her out as she tried to slink away. She went into a rage at me. If those fighters hadn't intervened, I think she would've torn me apart." Grandma Gert stopped and smiled at me as she picked up my bowl and spoon. "I just thought you might need to hear that story as you struggle with how you feel about your mother."

Maybe she understood more about my problems than I thought. "She was trying to protect you, right?"

She nodded. "Of course. Mothers want to protect their children. It's part of how our species survives. Some choose methods that damage us more than they save us. Don't mistake me, I'm glad to be alive. But the cost was high. High enough that I have sought to atone for my mother's sins every day of my life since then."

"What happened to her?" I didn't want to know the answer, but I couldn't stop myself from asking.

"The town decided to execute her for her betrayal, even though most of us would have died if not for that. They called it treason. Better to die for *liberté* than live as slaves and traitors. My father and I fled to try to put the past behind us. I'm not sure if things would've been better if they'd exiled her or jailed her until the war ended. Mostly, I'm grateful they didn't think my father and I deserved the same fate."

I paled. My mother loved me. I knew that without a doubt. She had a strange way of showing it, but she'd always acted to protect me. Execution for making the wrong choices to do that seemed...like the only thing they could do to save more lives in the middle of a war. We didn't have a war in Portland.

Except we kind of did. Petal Society and Rose Quarter had fought a war of sorts for a century. We—no, they—battled for the glory of winning ribbons and privileges and recognition at the Rose Festival and county fair, and a few other competitions. We even had a story about a disastrous rose blight caused by the feud.

According to Mom, the Rose Quarter coven had created this virulent disease and infected the entire city's rose population with it. They'd done it to get back at our coven for winning the grand prize in the three most coveted rose categories. The Petal Society had dealt with it and saved that year's festival.

Had my mom made a choice to somehow sacrifice me for that war? I remembered the crushing disappointment she'd shown after forcing my witch powers awake. Lying on my bed, crying and wishing for death, I'd heard my mother say something, and I couldn't forget it, no matter how hard

I'd tried.

"Wasted effort," she'd said, low enough that she might not have intended for me to hear her.

A few days later, Mom had taken me to the coven, begging for help.

"She's useless," I'd heard Mom say through a door. "Isn't there anything you can do?"

I hadn't heard the answer because I'd run for another room. Ashley had petted my hair, holding me while I cried again, and told me she'd watch over me.

"I won't let anyone hurt you," she'd murmured. Except the coven. For them, she had no trouble standing aside and letting them do whatever they wanted.

Sitting in Grandma Gert's dining room, I realized something for the first time. Ashley hadn't offered to help or try to teach me how to use what I had. She'd offered to stand in front of me and treat me like a fragile toy.

Mom had taught me how to control my power. The rest of the coven had taught me almost nothing else. At least, they hadn't taught me much on purpose. Most of what I knew had come from reading or seeing something and asking questions about it. They'd given me a basic grounding in the whole thing so I knew all the vocabulary and wouldn't cause any problems.

Grandma Gert patted my shoulder. "Trust your instincts. And good luck, Sophie. I have a feeling you'll need it."

Me too.

CHAPTER 16

Gabe and I lay side-by-side on the bed in the back room. He held the key's handle. Drew nestled between our knees, touching the key's teeth with his outstretched fingers. With luck, all three of us would face the rosebush together. I felt like I could handle it with their help.

The spot on my chest still felt weird, but I didn't know what to do about it. I didn't mention it. Why bother? The guys didn't know more than me.

"Your mom blasted it, so I guess that's what I'll do." Drew looked to me. "Any tips for doing that without hurting you guys with spillover?"

At this point, I had no idea why he still considered me his go-to expert. "I have no idea. I didn't even know we could do that."

"Right." Drew shifted his attention to the key.

I closed my eyes and gave my best shot at relaxing. We only had to somehow manage to defeat a rampaging rose monster that had almost killed me in seconds. What reason did I have to worry?

My mouth let out a weird sound like a strangled laugh. Then I landed in the cellar again. This time, Gabe landed beside me. Not Drew, though.

"Crap," Gabe muttered as he glanced around the room. He flashed me a forced smile. "I can probably handle a murderplant on my own."

"If I knew how to help, I would." I leaned against the correct shelf and shoved with all my strength.

Gabe joined me and shifted the shelf with little effort. "This would probably be a good time to start experimenting."

"Experimenting with what? My bare hands? Flinging around pathetic little wisps of power without controlling them?" My shoulders tightened and my neck hurt. I crouched over the lock with the key. "What if I make something terrible happen? What if I trigger something worse than the thing I already know about? What if—"

"Stop." Gabe set a firm hand on my shoulder. It felt like the strong grip of paternal authority and the gentle balm of warm comfort at the same time. "You're panicking. Instead of worrying about attacking it, worry about defending against it. It has thorns, right? Those thorns will scratch me just like they scratched you, so we need some shielding."

"Shielding." I knew the general principle. Sort of. "I know how to deflect an attack. Like, one attack. Not fifteen thrashing canes at once." Not that I'd managed to try last time. Fear had overwhelmed me. Like now.

"Forget about the canes."

"The canes almost killed me!"

Gabe sighed and rubbed his face.

I flung the key at the wall because I didn't know what to do.

"Sophie." He took both my hands in his and stared so hard at me it felt like a dare to meet his gaze. I couldn't. "Do you want to figure all this out or not? Does this matter to you or not?"

Instead of opening my mouth and shouting more panic at him, I snapped it shut and tried to breathe. When had I started crying? Why was I so useless?

"I understand. I really do. No one has ever expected you to do anything hard before. I know your mom well enough to guess that much. She treated you like a precious princess before you became a witch, right? Then when your power disappointed her, she shifted gears and you became more like a porcelain doll? And the other girls in the coven were your friends before, then they became your superiors? And you've never been the best at school, but you're pretty so everyone gives you a pass?"

He hit a little too close to home for my tastes. I sniffled and didn't respond.

"I'm on your side, Sophie, but you have to be honest if you want to deal with this stuff. Maybe you can rise above it once, but that won't solve anything in the long term."

Stung, I covered my face. If I could go back in time to before I met Drew, I thought I might do it. Even after everything that had happened, I still wanted that old life back. Without Drew, Mom would never have invaded my private sanctum. He and Claire would never have smashed my bedroom window.

I would never have met either of them. My life would suck, but in a way I understood. Like Cinderella, I had to choose between the crappy known and the terrifying unknown.

"I'm so pathetic."

"You're scared. It's okay to be scared. I'm scared too. I've never fought a rose monster before, and I don't know for sure that I can manage it. But I'm going to try anyway. Help me try, Sophie. Stop thinking about deflecting fifteen thorny canes and start thinking about protecting one squishy Gabe. A shield would work, or maybe something to make my aura solid?"

I blinked at him.

He smiled. "If you can manage it, a weapon would be great too."

Here. Now. Make a decision, Sophie. Do something. Stop being part of the problem and be part of the solution. You wanted this, right? Get off your ass and do it.

"I could, um..." What could I do? I scanned the room and saw a root cellar. The room had no weapons, shields, or armor. Of course it didn't. That would make our job too easy.

Like Gabe said, this was hard. Someone hid that key, and they'd done it for a reason.

"I could do a quick short-term enchantment on something, but I don't think I can make something out of power. I can't control enough of it at once."

My gaze hit the jam jars, of all things. I remembered dropping the one jar and how it had splashed everything. Adding magic gave me an idea. Pointing at their shelf, I said, "I could turn those into grenades."

Gabe straightened and grabbed one for me. "That's a start. How about..." He handed me the jar and checked bins. "Whatever this is?"

"A parsnip. That's a parsnip."

"No kidding?" He waved the long white root by its droopy green stalk. "I don't know what I thought parsnips looked like, but this wasn't it."

I giggled. Maybe he'd said that on purpose for me. "I guess I could... harden them?"

"I'll see what else I can find."

Gabe pawed through every bin and checked every shelf while I wrapped thin threads of energy around the outside of jam jars, like hand-winding a bobbin for a sewing machine. Every moment, I had to focus on what I wanted the power to do. On impact, I wanted it to constrict then expand, to shatter the jar and fling the shards of glass in every direction with a little magical boost in sharpness.

As I finished with the fourth one, Gabe slammed his elbow through a board with a crack loud enough to hurt my ears. He rubbed his arm and brandished the makeshift club he'd made.

"What can you do with this?"

I took the jagged piece of wood and found it heavier than expected. He'd picked a good piece. If I could've turned it into a machete, it would've served us well. But I couldn't imagine how to do that. Instead, I chose to use the same approach as with the jam grenades.

"Make it more solid, like steel. But not sharp like a blade."

He shrugged. "At this point, anything is better than nothing."

As I wrapped threads around the club, I realized Gabe probably had no idea how metaphysical spaces worked. I had plenty to learn still, but I'd been inside them a few times.

"Where we're going, how much you want something is more important than your muscle strength or speed."

"Sure," he nodded, "because it's all in our heads. We'll need to think our way to victory. Which is why you didn't win before. You didn't think you could."

My cheeks burned.

"And you still don't."

"It's not that, I just—"

"It's okay, Sophie." He picked up a jam grenade and examined it. "When I step onto the soccer field, I know losing is a possibility. It's inevitable we'll lose some games. But I don't go out there thinking about how we might lose. I go out there knowing we have a serious chance of winning."

In other words, Sophie, pull your head out of your ass, stop crying, and do your job. I tied off the enchantment on the club and handed it to him. "I'll protect you as much as I can," I mumbled. Had I ever blushed this fiercely before? Probably not.

"No. You'll protect me." Gabe dropped a jam grenade into his pocket and kept the other in his hand. "Because the alternative is we both die."

I gulped and slipped one jam grenade into each pocket. Maybe Drew would save us, but so what? That didn't get us anywhere. Nothing changed if we didn't figure out why the key opened a metaphysical realm and why that mattered to my mom.

Nodding, I fetched the key again. "I'll protect you."

Hopefully.

CHAPTER 17

I opened the lock. Gabe took my hand as the door opened. We jumped through the green glow together. The moment I landed on the street, I hefted a jam grenade. Gabe raised his club.

"Is that it?" He pointed up the street at a dark smudge.

"Probably." I would not panic. I would not abandon Gabe.

"Focus on defense."

Right. Sure. Just like that.

"Stop watching it get closer. Stay behind me and stare at my back."

I followed orders. Doing so had served me well all my life. Because I was a coward. If I'd ever had an ounce of courage, I would've stood up to Mom.

The street trembled. I didn't have time for this. If I didn't do something, the rosebush would cut us up. We'd fail and nothing would change. I wanted things to change. I needed things to change.

Think, Sophie. How would I make armor from nothing without making armor from nothing? If I had something, I could bolster it.

The shrubbery rustled its leaves in an eerie roar.

Gabe's power affected water. My power had a water affinity. I could use that, but how? "Can you summon water to your body to absorb blows?"

"There's no water here." Gabe hurled his grenade. I handed him one of mine.

The rosebush screeched like a horde of angry, demonic crickets. My bones vibrated in response. I cringed. Gabe squirmed and grunted. His shirt shifted as his muscles moved.

Gabe wore a shirt. A shirt, by definition, was something. Jeans also qualified. I could bolster his clothes. Way to go, Sophie, good job on thinking of something useful at the last possible moment, when I had almost zero chance of holding my concentration. For a follow-up, I could try throwing my other grenade at Gabe's head and see if that helped the situation.

"Don't jump. I'm going to touch you."

"I mentioned I'm gay, right?"

At a time like this, he thought I wanted to grab his butt or something? I smacked my palms on his back after he threw another grenade. "Try not to move too much."

The rose monster shrieked again.

"It's not closing the distance." Gabe held the third grenade ready.

"I wouldn't either if someone kept throwing pain at my face."

"These were a good idea."

That simple compliment made me glow. It shouldn't have, but it did. When had Mom last complimented me on something besides my looks? When had anyone besides Drew done that? Never? Four years ago?

Why did I fixate on the little things at a time like this? "Hold still. And stop talking to me. I have to concentrate."

I focused on his aura. The deep, dark blue surrounding him rippled into focus. Flowing freely over his entire body, it reminded me of Drew. These boys commanded so much power compared to me, yet I held all the keys. Claire and I had that in common, I supposed. She had Drew wrapped around her little finger so tight I wondered how he could breathe sometimes. And he liked it.

Gabe threw the third grenade. The rose monster squealed. I handed him the last one.

Focus, Sophie. Gabe's aura meshed with mine in an instant thanks to our binding. We should've experimented before hopping through the door. Never mind that. Stay on target.

Pulling power from Drew, I draped thick streamers over Gabe's shirt. As I did so, I realized I could bolster his aura instead of his shirt. Of course I could do that. In a metaphysical realm, his shirt didn't exist. Duh.

Through me, the power could only flow so fast. It swirled over Gabe like soft serve ice cream.

"I can feel that," he murmured.

I glanced up and regretted it. The rose monster shivered out of reach, watching us. Red jam dripped from canes and leaves with slashes across them. Small cuttings lay on the ground. Instead of blood, the broken parts oozed clear, sap-like liquid. Before I turned away, it lunged toward us.

My entire being flinched, cowered, and squeaked. Gabe threw the last grenade. With my eyes shut, I could only cringe at its piteous, hideous wail.

"I guess that'll have to do." Gabe abandoned me and rushed the rose monster.

Without him, I felt suddenly naked. I wanted to curl into a ball and cover myself with something more than my coat. But I forced myself to try to keep bolstering him despite the distance. He'd come to this awful place to help me, not the other way around.

This quest belonged to me, and I needed to remember that. I needed to live that truth. Gabe and Drew only put themselves in danger for my sake.

Because they loved me, I guess.

I reached for the binding with Gabe, visualizing it as a silvery blue cord between us. Another cord disappeared into the distance, linking me with Drew. Why didn't Gabe have a second cord connecting him directly to Drew? No idea. Maybe because I'd directed the process?

Forcing myself to watch, I slipped my hands into Gabe's aura.

Not really. I did it from a distance, like using a VR headset. Instead of touching it, I directed the extension of myself that connected to him by moving my hands. Physical gestures made the mental process easier to cling to and direct.

The rose slashed its canes. I shifted the power to cover that part of Gabe. He whacked the plant monster with his club.

Intent on following the canes threatening Gabe, I had no idea what traced a line of pure agony up the back of my calf. I gasped and looked down. The wretched thing had spawned a miniature clone, tall enough to reach my knees.

Tiny canes with tiny leaves wrapped around my leg, slapping tiny thorns through my jeans to pierce my skin.

Without thinking, I squeaked and stomped it with my other foot. Canes crunched. Thank goodness I had real shoes, because the thorns didn't pierce the rubber soles deep enough to reach my feet.

It roared and rustled, the tiny sound almost cute compared to the bigger plant.

I didn't have an actual weapon. Gabe had one, but he had his own thorns to worry about. If I couldn't handle my own tiny adversary, we had bigger problems than rampaging rose monsters. My foot had worked once, though.

I stomped it again. Branches snapped. Canes flailed.

To my genuine surprise, my shoe worked as an effective weapon against a miniature rose monster. Every stomp reduced its menace quotient by a lot. The little plant didn't stand a chance. I reduced it to a twitching pile of roots and damaged canes surrounded by a scattering of fallen leaves and buds.

My efforts had accomplished something. I'd killed a thing that wanted to kill me. With my foot. Did it really matter that I couldn't do much with magic? Gabe played soccer without it. Drew understood calculus without it. Claire punched things in the face without it.

Mom had convinced me that I couldn't do anything because I couldn't do one thing. Or had I convinced myself? Did it matter?

Flush with victory, I raised my head to tell Gabe about my success.

He still fought the bigger rosebush. How had I not noticed? The moment I'd discovered my tiny attacker, nothing else had mattered. Because I'm a selfish brat, I guess.

My vision had reverted, so I couldn't see his aura or the armor I'd draped over it. I could see a cane hitting him and forcing him to stagger back a step. I could also see him having a hard time recovering from the attack.

Rushing in wouldn't help. The rosebush would slash me to ribbons. Unless I covered myself in the same armor I'd put over Gabe. Affecting me instead of him meant I didn't have to shift my vision, which meant I could do it faster.

I closed my eyes, took a deep breath, and firmed the outer edge of my aura. The power flowed from Drew to me in a steady stream, giving me as much as I could manage.

Gabe grunted with an edge of pain. I couldn't delay any longer.

Certain I'd done everything I could, I opened my eyes and charged the rose monster. My aura would hold. It had to. Drew bolstered it, so it couldn't fail.

As I reached him, Gabe groaned and his body crumpled to one side. A spray of red filled the air. I leaped. My body crashed into a huge pile of canes. Branches snapped. It squalled like a frightened sheep made of leaves and sticks.

I'd taken a chance, and I hurt it! This thing that had almost killed me lay in a thrashing heap under my body, crying in pain.

Victory tasted...weird.

CHAPTER 18

I scrambled to my feet and kicked the plant. Gabe whacked it with his club. The thing dragged itself away, leaving us in peace. Wary of a trick, I watched it while Gabe panted to catch his breath and held his side.

"Thanks," Gabe said. "I don't know that I could've finished it without your help."

"Are you okay?" I wasn't usually the person who asked that question. My head spun.

"It got me a few times, but not too bad. You?"

As soon as he asked, the cuts on my calf flared with sharp, stinging pain. "Just my leg. I'll be fine so long as we don't have to run."

"Same, I think."

The rose monster kept wriggling away, so I ignored it. "It was so hard before, but seemed so easy this time."

"Attitude makes a big difference. Also, those grenades hurt it and made it more careful. The thing learned. Which is kind of terrifying. Whoever made it knew what they were doing."

I wondered if they'd negotiated with it somehow instead of making it. Not that it mattered. We'd beaten it. On to the next problem. "Now we just have to figure out what else is here."

"Oh, is that all?" Gabe grinned and waved in both directions. "Which way do you want to go?"

"The rose monster went that way, so let's go the other way."

"Hard to argue with that logic."

Though I had no hope of supporting him, I ducked under his arm to help him. Gabe slipped his hand around my waist. We leaned on each other.

Shambling up the road together, we split the duty of watching for something without having to say anything. I kept an eye to the right, and he did the left. Nothing seemed special about anything in particular. The trees waved in a gentle breeze filled with rose musk and sawdust, the sun formed whimsical shapes on the ground, and the old-fashioned buildings refused to focus through the mist.

I remembered the icky, foreboding doorway and hoped we found something else to investigate.

"That's different," Gabe said.

Of course it was the doorway of doom. I sighed when I saw that he pointed at it. "There must be another option."

"I'm sure the spider responsible for those thick webs is friendly."

Ugh. I grimaced and hunched my shoulders. He steered me toward it. The closer we shuffled, the weaker the sunshine became. Thin, sickly light cast a grotesque pall over the cobweb barrier between two puke-yellow, drooping birches.

Gabe poked the webbing with his club. The strands rippled like water. "It's almost like someone doesn't want us to go here."

"It's working."

"Bah. That rosebush had at least a dozen branches. A giant spider only has eight legs and two fangs."

"You're assuming it's a giant spider." I wanted to stop and refuse to go through there. At this point, I didn't think I'd ever again get what I wanted. "Swipe that stuff aside so we can go find the spider and discover this is the wrong way already."

Chuckling, Gabe stabbed the webbing with his club. The strands tore easily and stuck to the wood. I stuck my hand into the mess and found the web threads rough. They caught on everything, including skin. Within seconds, we both had trails of wispy white crap fluttering around us.

I tried wiping the strands on my jeans, which made them split apart so I had threads stuck to my hands and my jeans. Gabe whacked the tree with his club, managing to shift some of the stuff to the leaves and branches. Wiping my hand on a tree trunk didn't help, though. Bits of bark peeled off and snagged in the webs, making my problem worse.

"This is stupid," I grumbled.

"You're a witch. Do something witchy."

"You're a river god's son. Do something river goddy."

"Like what? River gods don't make water. We control it and commune with fish and stuff."

Huffing in annoyance, I swatted the strands. Movement above caught my eyes. I looked up. "I found the giant spiders," I whimpered.

Two huge white spiders, each bigger than Gabe, leaped from the tree canopy to attack us. Out of a reflex I didn't know I had, I raised my hands and spewed power. But I needed more time. The thing moved too fast for me to do anything other than move.

To my surprise, time seemed to slow around me. The spider leaped. Its legs shifted forward. I saw individual hairs on its snowy body, pushed back by the wind of its passage. So many glittering pink eyes pointed at me.

With every moment that passed in this bizarre, slow-motion version of reality, another layer of protection bolstered my shield. The power seemed to flow faster than it should. Had I done something to slow the spider? No, that didn't make sense. Magic couldn't affect the flow of time.

So my coven had taught me. By now, I knew better than to believe what they'd said, didn't I?

The spider hit a barrier the size of my aura and bounced to the side. I staggered under the weight without falling. My shield shattered.

I'd deflected an attack! By myself! With only a split-second of warning! By slowing time! Or something like that!

I stared, stunned. The spider wobbled and clicked, and found its feet. Right. It still wanted to eat me. Unwilling to take my attention off it to check Gabe, I focused on bolstering the barrier around my body. The front needed more than the back.

My spider charged. I braced for impact, leaning forward with my hands in front of me. Its charge slowed again, as if it ran through thick water. That thing would hit me with even more force this time. If I did nothing more than shield myself, would it learn like the rosebush had? Probably.

Not sure if it would work, I brought my hands together and forced the barrier to a point. It formed a long, sharp edge in front of me. With every passing moment, I threw more and more power at the shape. At the blade. Made of my will, my power, and my unexpected capability.

The spider leaped. I kept pouring in the power. It hit my shield. The blade edge sliced through the spider's body, cutting it in half and showering me with sulfurous gore. High-pitched, wailing shrieks filled the air. Briefly.

Time returned to normal. Two halves of a giant spider twitched at my feet. I wiped goopy green crap from my face.

By myself, I'd taken out a giant spider intent on killing me. No one else had done this. The way I'd done it seemed so natural and logical, yet I'd never considered anything like it before.

If I ignored everything I'd ever learned about magic, I could make up my own rules and test them. Experimentation would serve as a better teacher than the Petal Society ever had. To hell with them. To hell with their rules. To hell with their everything.

I looked up and saw Gabe pinned by the other spider, his club gripped in its mandibles. He held it off for the moment but definitely needed help. What had worked for the rosebush could work for a spider, I figured. My shield remained intact from the other spider.

Did I have any other ideas? No, I sure didn't.

Feeling like a superhero on a righteous mission for glorious valor, I ran and jumped at the spider. Time once again seemed to slow, making the spider fail to react in time. It lifted one leg into my path.

The blade remained on the front of my barrier. I sheared off the spider's leg at an odd angle. My shield crashed into the spider, slicing across its body. As we fell, the shield failed. I hit the spider. The spider hit Gabe. Green goo soaked us both. We stank like a pile of rotten eggs.

Yuck.

Gabe lay on the ground, panting and holding his club. I shoved at the split corpse. It wobbled without budging. The legs waved in the air.

Sophie the amazing spider slayer couldn't lift her kills to save her life, or anyone else's.

I giggled.

Gabe spat green muck and wriggled himself free of the corpse. Once he'd freed himself, I helped him stand. My coat steamed itself clean, though that didn't help the rest of me.

"That was...something. It was really something."

My giggles faded. "I didn't know I could do any of what I just did."

"I'm glad you figured it out before that spider ripped off my arm. I don't suppose you can figure out how to get this gunk off us? Spider guts are pretty gross." He flung his hand, spattering goo on the ground.

Using my coat sleeve to wipe his arm helped, though it didn't take care of all the muck. "Maybe, but I'd rather get this over with. There won't be any spider goo outside this place."

Gabe sighed and nodded. "Fine, let's keep moving." He swished his club through the remaining webs. The threads sloughed off the end. At least the spider guts kept the webs from sticking to us.

Through the doorway, we found a dark, dank brick tunnel. Gabe took a step to lead the way. I wanted to call myself stupid for doing so, but I put a hand on his shoulder.

"I'll go first," my dumb mouth said.

He raised his brow. "You sure?"

Not exactly. I nodded anyway. "Yes. I'm sure." Rawr.

CHAPTER 19

Three steps into the tunnel, I raised a hand and made a soft blue light. That, at least, I knew I could do without issue. Ashley had taught me how to do it once when we had a sleepover. At the time, I'd been grateful for the lesson. Thinking over it now, I realized she'd wanted me to expend my power so she could conserve her own.

After all, what difference did it make if Sophie blew her magic? It wasn't like I could do anything more useful.

Anger bubbled in my gut. I could do plenty. If they'd given me a chance, they would've seen that. I would've known it four years ago instead of learning it today. But no, Sophie is useless.

The coven could take that "useless" and stick it in a giant spider corpse.

I hated them. All of them. Every last member of the coven had done something to me that I wanted to avenge. Some things seemed too petty to deserve hate. I hated them anyway. The moment any of them did one more thing to me, I was ready to declare my own war on the Petal Society and burn it all down around them.

The Rose Quarter could die in flames too, for all I cared. They'd done something terrible to Gabe, and I had no doubt they would've treated me exactly the same as Petal Society if I'd been born to one of them instead.

"You're stomping," Gabe said.

"What?" I whirled and shoved my light in his face.

He flinched and held up his hands in surrender.

His reaction made me want to crawl into a hole and die. Gabe didn't deserve any of my hate or anger. "Sorry," I mumbled as I turned my back on him again.

"It's okay. I get weird after a game sometimes. Like, you find this amazing freedom and joy, then it all comes crashing down once the game ends and you have to go home again. Life roars back whether you want it or not. I guess that's why I liked going to Witch's Castle on Friday nights. It felt like a different world, a different life. An escape. Sort of. I mean, I had to pretend I was interested in the girls, so it wasn't all sunshine and laughs, but it was better than being at home."

"That's so messed up." I ran my fingers along the brick wall, wondering if we had to look for a hidden door or something. The tunnel kept going and going. Damp dirt carried a vague whiff of rotting meat. Copper or another metal hung in the air, thick enough to taste.

"I guess I owe you some thanks for finding a reason to quit your coven. It probably won't matter, though. Mom will just want me to try to date Ashley instead."

"Why did she pick me anyway? I mean, if she wanted you to make witch babies, Ashley seems like the better option." Bitterness left an acidic taste in my mouth.

Gabe sighed. "I think you can probably guess the reason."

I bared my teeth. "No one paid attention to me, so you'd have an easier time getting information."

"Yeah."

Yes, I hated all of them. Catty, rude, evil witches had ruined my life from every angle. All these women felt some wretched need to beat each other at rose growing contests. That sounded like the stupidest reason imaginable to cause so much harm and pain. Because of them, I had no friends outside the coven, so I hadn't had a reprieve until I met Drew. Ever.

Ahead, a flicker of candlelight caught my attention. Thank goodness, because my thoughts had dipped into a dark place. "Do you see that?" As I asked, I spun power into my shields.

"Yes. I wonder if it's supposed to distract us?" He tapped his club against the bricks on our right side as we walked.

"Probably. It's pretty clear whoever built this didn't want anyone getting in here."

"Why did they build it, then? I mean, why bother?"

I shrugged. Then I realized I knew the answer. "The same reason your mom keeps that key in a place that's hard to find and get at. To protect something. Right? If you have a precious thing or a dangerous thing, and you want to keep it, you protect it. I'm betting it's dangerous or my mom wouldn't want it."

"What would your mom want?"

We neared the source of the light, an actual candle burning with an actual flame. "I don't know."

"I barely know her, but my guess is power."

I had no reason to refute him. Except the answer seemed off. Yes, Mom liked power, but she always used it. She never wasted or frittered it. If she wanted a lot of power, she wanted it for a reason, not just to have it. "I keep wondering what she was doing in the woods."

"Something that attracted the node's attention. I don't know how hard that is, so I don't have any ideas."

"Maybe we should ask Portland some questions before we go back there."

Gabe snorted. "I'm sure we'll suddenly get lots of non-cryptic, really helpful answers."

"It doesn't hurt to ask," I muttered.

We reached a dead end. The candle, a cream wax taper, sat on a silvery metal saucer in a small recess in the wall. Its flame threw simple, wavering shadows on the bricks. A quick check didn't reveal any seams other than the mortar between bricks, and none seemed likely to mark the edges of a door.

I frowned at the candle. "Now what?"

Gabe reached past me and picked up the candle. It popped off the small plate. Nothing else happened.

Peering at the plate, I couldn't place what seemed weird about it. I stared at the thing for what seemed like a long time before I realized it had no obvious way to have held the candle in place. The plate had no wax pool, depression, or spike. How had it stood on the plate, and why had Gabe needed to tug to pop it free?

The flame continued to burn. Gabe tipped it on its side and wax ran down the taper's length. He fiddled with it, melting the wax and letting a drop fall to the ground. It formed a flattened blob on the dirt, like any other fallen wax would do anywhere else.

I poked the plate. My fingernail clinked against what felt like sturdy yet thin steel. "Drip some wax on the plate. I want to see what happens."

Nodding, Gabe held the candle over the plate. A drop of wax fell. It hit the plate with a clink like a pair of crystals tumbling together. The drop bounced and formed a perfect sphere. We glanced at each other. He found the noise as weird as I did.

More wax fell onto the plate, creating more tiny spheres. Though I wanted to keep watching, I remembered the spiders waiting for us to get distracted.

I checked behind us. Nothing. The clinking echoed into the distance.

"They're multiplying."

Turning back, I saw dozens of tiny spheres dividing to form more and more tiny spheres. When they covered the surface of the saucer, the candle flared.

Gabe swore and dropped the taper. He shook out his hand and hissed, stepping away from the plate and behind me to suck on his finger. "It burned me."

The candle hit the plate and tipped it. All the tiny spheres flew into the air. Torn between an impulse to catch them and curiosity, I watched, transfixed as the tiny spheres reached the top of their bounce and hovered there. The flame died. In the dim glow of my blue light, the wax balls fell and shattered the plate into a thousand shards.

Tiny, sharp pieces of metal, streaking white hot, shot at my face. They hit my shield. Then they fell to the ground.

In my whole life, I had never been as grateful for anything as the thought to bolster that shield before we'd reached this point.

My shield dimpled under the stress, but with Drew's inexhaustible well feeding it, not a single shard passed through to hit me or Gabe. Drew had saved our lives.

"I guess that was a trap?" Gabe said as he peered over my shoulder.

I nudged shards with my shoe. They didn't leap into the air to launch a second assault. "Seems like it. What did they guard, though?"

"Check the shelf? I'm going to hide behind your shield."

The idea of Gabe, the big, strong, athletic guy, hiding behind me made me want to burst into laughter. I smothered a grin and reached out a hand to prod the recess in the wall. At the touch of my shields, the bricks shoved aside and fell to the ground. They revealed a small, dark hole.

Inside the hole, I found a small wooden box, the right size to hold an engagement ring. I reached into the hole and picked it up. A dark iron plate with an odd-shaped depression covered half the box. The seams suggested we had to find a way to remove the plate. After squinting at it for a few seconds, I figured it out.

"I think we need your mom's key to open this."

CHAPTER 20

Opening my eyes, I smiled at Grandma Gert's back room. My head hurt enough to notice. Compared to my previous experience, this felt like nothing.

Gabe groaned and sat up, holding his head. "I officially hate roses, spiders, and candles."

"No kidding."

Drew sat at the foot of the bed, watching us with a curious expression I couldn't translate. He definitely seemed relieved, but did he also seem a little jealous? "I'm glad you're both okay. About ten seconds ago, the key flared with light and disappeared."

I raised my hand, no longer wrapped around the key. Instead, I held the box. My fingers spasmed with cramps, so I tossed the box to Drew and shook out my hand.

"Interesting keyhole." Of course Drew figured that out within half a second of seeing it.

"Now we just have to figure out how to get my mom's key," Gabe said. "I'm sure it'll be easy, like strolling down a street."

Unable to help myself, I laughed.

"You should've seen Sophie. She was amazing." Gabe told Drew everything while I giggled like a lunatic.

I'd done all those things. Even if they hadn't happened in the real, live world, I'd still done them. The worthless, pathetic waste of a disappointment had kicked butt and protected the boy. Having succeeded there, I knew I could face down my mom.

With help. I probably needed help, but I wouldn't falter. Anne and Stace had made a huge mistake in sending me after that key.

"That's amazing." Drew tucked the box into his pocket and slid off the bed. "We should get moving." He offered me a hand.

I took his help and kept my hold on his hand as we left the room. Grandma Gert sat in the next room with a plate of cookies on the small table beside her. She tapped it.

"Take one or two for the road."

"Thank you, Grandma Gert. I'm sorry to eat and run, but we're kind of in a hurry now." Drew crossed the room with me in tow and kissed her cheek.

"I really appreciate your help." I took a cookie. Then I took a second one because she said we could.

"When I told you my home is always open to you, I meant it. Even if you only need a port in a storm for a few hours. Go take care of the things you need to take care of." She patted Drew's hand and winked at me.

On the way out, Drew and Gabe each took two cookies for themselves. We all munched and crunched as we left through the front door. Though we all knew where we needed to go, we needed a plan first, so we'd decided to walk up the street and figure it out.

Grandma Gert lived on a charming little street full of squat one-story houses with low fences around winterized gardens. Rhododendrons hunched everywhere, and leafless trees lined the parking strips. Mailboxes painted like dogs, cats, pigs, cows, and other animals perched on fence posts.

Gabe opened the gate for us and led us to the left.

I squeezed Drew's hand as we headed up the sidewalk. "I know you had a lot of crappy foster homes. Why couldn't you stay with Grandma Gert? She's so nice."

Drew opened his mouth to answer. He stumbled. His hand released mine, and his eyes fluttered shut. Nothing I saw made sense until I turned and saw my mom. She yanked her hand back and Drew flew to her. Then she wrapped a hand around his neck.

Frozen in terror, I couldn't breathe. She'd taken him by surprise, which meant she could do anything to him. If she didn't snap his neck, she could force her way into his private sanctum and do anything. Unless the node protected him, which it might.

"Don't hurt him," I whimpered.

Gabe clutched my shoulders as if to keep me from rushing her or running away. He didn't need to bother. I couldn't move.

Mom glared at me. "Where's the key?"

"It's gone." Even if I wanted to lie to her, I couldn't.

"Gone where?"

"We don't know," Gabe said.

Mom narrowed her eyes at Gabe. She could see his aura now. Whether she knew what it meant, I couldn't say. But she could see it. "If you want to see Drew again, you're going to find it and bring it to me."

"Mom, what are you doing?" Why did I still believe she loved me? Why did I want her to?

"You have four hours. Bring it to that place in the forest, with the rosebush. If you don't show up with the key, Drew dies. His blood will be on your hands." She dragged him to a car I should've seen on the way out of Grandma Gert's house.

Why hadn't I seen her car? How could I have missed it? She drove a white minivan that never stood out, but I should've noticed it. We could've prepared for her.

"You could rush her with your shield active," Gabe whispered in my ear.

For a wild moment, I saw myself doing it. Then I shook my head because reality popped the fantasy like a soap bubble. "She'll kill him." Drew's death would kill me. It would kill Claire. "I believe she'll do it."

Maybe she wouldn't kill me, but I knew in my heart she would kill Drew if she thought it would get her what she wanted.

Gabe and I watched my mother abduct my best friend, unable to prevent it. She drove away from us with Drew under her magical control.

A gentle breeze tousled my bangs. Shivers wriggled down my spine. My eyes itched with the need to cry. Heat flared in my cheeks.

"This is my fault," I whispered.

"No." Gabe hugged me from behind. "This is her fault. She's responsible for her own actions. And she's the adult."

"What do I do? Drew is so much more powerful than me, and she took him down in a second!"

"We." Gabe kept a firm grip on me without making me feel trapped. "I'm not going to stand by and watch while that bitch kills Drew, so you better count me in on this. And the first thing we need to do is figure out where we are."

Drew had brought us here, and I didn't have the power to replicate his mode of travel. I couldn't even do that with his help. The process used more energy than I could control. Unless the node decided to yank us to its side, we had to use mundane transportation. Even worse, I didn't have a way to contact or reach Claire without him, so I couldn't get her help.

Gabe let go of me to take my hand. "Come on." He dragged me back to Grandma Gert's front door and knocked.

She answered with a raised brow and a friendly smile. "Did you forget something?"

"No. Sophie's mom just attacked and took Drew. I need to know where we are. He brought us here with— I mean, neither of us was paying attention on the way. We're kind of lost now."

Grandma Gert frowned, and I saw a flicker of angry fire in it. "Come back inside and do whatever you need."

Gabe led me inside. My mind whirled while he talked to Grandma Gert. We couldn't get the key for Mom. She didn't know that. Would she search Drew and find the box in his pocket? Assuming she did, giving her the other key sounded like a terrible idea. Did we have some other choice? Mom would know it if we gave her a fake key.

"We have to get your mom's key," I whispered.

"I agree. Just a minute." Gabe held up a hand as Grandma Gert spread a paper map over her dining room table.

She pointed to a spot on the map in Oak Grove, a suburb southeast of Portland. The node had sent us to a forest in on the northeast side of Troutdale. It would've taken Mom less than an hour to cross the distance in her car. I didn't know how much time either of my trips into the key's metaphysical space had taken, let alone Gabe's healing dunk, but I expected at least an hour, if not two or three.

But how had Mom known where to find us? Since she hadn't popped up at random before this, I didn't think she could track Drew's method of travel. I didn't have my phone, so if she had a way to use it to find me, it wouldn't have worked. She hadn't known about Gabe's aura until two minutes ago, so she couldn't have done anything based on him. From past experience, I knew she couldn't track my aura.

I noticed myself rubbing the spot on my chest where she'd blasted me. The skin there still itched enough to annoy me. My fingers rubbed over my focus stone.

She'd blasted me in the chest. Where I wore my focus stone.

I yanked the chain to get it out of my shirt and coat. The moment it stopped touching my flesh, I stopped feeling that weird itch. The blue stone, an opaque teardrop riddled with silvery lines, had been a gift from my mother. According to her, our ancestor, Jacqueline, had made it in the early 1900s. Did I believe her anymore?

No. I didn't believe a word of the story she'd told me.

Somehow, her blasting my stone had given her a way to track me, and I wanted nothing to do with it, ever again. I snapped the clasp and glared at the stone dangling from its silver chain. The thing worked, I knew that much.

It did its job of making magic easier for me to use. The first time Drew had seen it, he'd coveted it, so I knew it could do even more for him than it did for me.

Given some time to sit and work without interruption or innocent kids nearby, we could make me a new one. At the moment, getting rid of my most important tool seemed stupid. But I couldn't use it anymore. Especially if it gave Mom even the slightest edge when facing me.

On the off chance my ancestor had actually made it, I set the stone on the table. "Grandma Gert, can you keep this for me? I think my mom is using it to track me. I might feel safe taking it again later, but right now, I can't risk it."

"Of course. I'll put it someplace safe." She smiled at me and patted my hand.

Gabe folded the map. "My car is nowhere near here, which cuts our options to move fast. I do have one possibility, though, so we're going to try that. If it doesn't work, I don't know what our next move will be, but we'll think of something."

He wanted me to have hope.

I tried. I really, really tried.

CHAPTER 21

We ran down the street. My breathing settled into a rhythm, and I had no problem keeping up with Mr. Soccer Player. Gabe yanked me around a corner to a narrower street. At the end of this street, I saw the glimmer of sunshine on water.

"Where are we going?" I had a terrible feeling I knew the answer.

"To the Willamette."

An icy knife of fear lodged in my gut. "I can't swim."

"You won't have to."

He had some plan, and it involved the river. I hated this plan without knowing anything else about it.

"But it's a river."

"And I'm the son of a river god."

"I'm a witch. I can't go in the water like that. I'll drown. I don't want to drown." Did I sound hysterical? Maybe a little?

"I promise you won't drown. I can't promise anything else, but I know for a fact you will not drown. The water won't disintegrate you, either. You'll be fine. Trust me."

Famous last words. "But—"

"Sophie." He squeezed my hand. Even after spending less than a day with him, I already associated that gesture with comfort and care. "Can you trust me over your mom in this?"

"I don't trust my mom."

He glanced at me with a raised eyebrow.

"Okay, fine, I don't know what to trust or not trust with my mom. I don't know how much she lied to me and how much was true. I don't even know if anything my mom or the coven taught me works like they said. The point is, that's water, and I don't know how to swim."

Saying those things out loud seemed more concrete than thinking them. I didn't want to stop saying things like that.

"I hate my mom. I hate her so much it's tearing me apart inside. Like there's an alien in my gut trying to burst free. She's not the person I thought she was, and I'm not the person I thought I was, and I just want to go home and not have to stop her from killing the first person who ever cared about me for me instead of for what I could be or failed to become."

Gabe stopped and whipped me into a hug. I hit his chest and would've bounced off his wall of muscle if he hadn't held me close. His whole body heaved as he breathed deep to catch his breath. So did mine.

"I know you're scared. It's okay to be scared. I'm not really scared right this minute because I have a plan. I figured it'd be faster if we just put my plan into motion than if I take the time to explain it. But you've had a rough day, and it's fair that you're not up for more."

Great. Now I'd slowed us down on top of everything else. When Mom called me useless, she was right. If I didn't have Gabe to help me, I didn't think I could handle this. Four hours? Why did Mom think I could get the key and get to Troutdale from Oak Grove in four hours without a car? Had she gone insane?

"What's not fair is that we can't stop now. Drew needs us. If we don't deliver, I think you're right that your mom won't have any trouble killing Drew. Even worse, I think she's going to do it anyway. I can picture us handing over the key and her slashing Drew's throat as she throws him at us."

I gasped. Mom double-crossing us hadn't even occurred to me. It probably would have eventually. If we'd kept going at a breakneck pace, worrying about the key and nothing more, I might not have thought of it until too late.

"So we're going to get some help. But we have to move fast to get it, and without my car, I've only got one option for speed."

"The river."

He nodded. "The river. I can swim like a freaking otter on crack, and I can carry you with me. You won't drown. I promise you will not drown. I promise it won't hurt. Will you let me carry you down the river?"

I couldn't quite process everything he said. The words flowed around me, not making sense and yet making sense at the same time. My brain buzzed with a cloud of panic for Drew. I imagined trying to explain to Claire what had happened. She yelled at me for not telling her. I had no way to do it! Without Drew, I had no way to reach her!

Numb, confused, terrified, ashamed, and facing a tidal wave of guilt crashing over me, I nodded.

Gabe jerked me into another run. We plunged past the end of the asphalt, where the road narrowed to a rocky dirt path. Trees on both sides leaned toward us, forming a canopy to block the waning afternoon sunshine. Water glittered before us.

He kept going. I stumbled over the rocks in his wake, still chained to his progress by his hand around my wrist.

At the water's edge, he turned to face me and tapped next to his eye. "Look at my face. Don't look at the water. Focus on me. Hold onto me and don't let go. I'm going to keep you safe. You're going to get wet, but nothing else bad will happen. Your coat will be fine, and so will you. When we get out of the river, I'll dry you off."

He stepped into the water. I gulped and hesitated at the edge where the water lapped against the mud and stones.

"What if I can't hold on?"

"Here." He let go, turned around, and offered his hands over his shoulders. "Hold onto my neck."

"How will I breathe? Will I be underwater?"

"You're stalling. I made you a promise, Sophie. I'm going to keep it."

Lots of people had made me lots of promises. "Have you ever done this before?"

"Yes."

"With who?"

He threw an exasperated glare over his shoulder. "Sophie. I'm not your mom or a member of that coven. I admit I originally lied to you quite a bit because my mom made me, but I've been honest with you today, one hundred percent. We're going to save Drew. This is step one. We can't do step two if you can't trust me."

I could do this. Drew needed me to do this. Gabe, who I trusted, would keep me safe. "Okay."

My heart pounding, I took his hands.

"Close your eyes. It might also help if you take a deep breath and keep your mouth shut for a few seconds." He bent his knees and tugged my arms until I pressed against him and my head rested on his shoulder. "Hold on to your own arms around my neck. It'll make things easier for me."

I followed directions, gripping my forearms with both hands. Trust. Gabe had asked for my trust, and I gave it to him. Not because he demanded it, but because he deserved it. Because Drew deserved my willingness to take a risk for him.

Gabe waded into the water. I screwed shut my eyes and took a deep breath. He jumped. For a moment, I flew. Then we hit the frigid water with a smooth, barely audible splash. Water engulfed us. The cold shocked me.

His body rippled, undulating like a wave. The water rushed past. My body fell into a rhythm with his, rising and falling as his did. We cut through the water like a single being. His warmth blazed against my chest and belly, chasing away my chill.

When I couldn't hold my breath anymore, when I thought my lungs might explode, I took a breath. I expected water to rush into my mouth. It didn't. Bright light flashed against my eyelids. As soon as I closed my mouth again, the light faded.

Gabe had said to keep my eyes closed, but I had to see. Peeking through a tight squint, I saw a world of deep blue-green. Shapes flashed past too fast to comprehend. We broke the surface as I breathed in. Sunshine dazzled me. The wind pressed against my face. Trees on the shore blurred together in smudges of green and brown.

Then we dove beneath again, into the murky depths. Dark shapes flitted past too fast to track. I opened my mouth and we speared upward, breaking out of the water like a rocket. Instead of annoying Gabe, I took as a deep a breath as I could and held it. He didn't need to leap out of the water every two seconds for me.

Surrounded by wonder, I closed my eyes and snugged my body tighter against him. Another day, when we could take our time, I'd ask him to take me swimming again. For now, I didn't want to distract him too much, and I did want to get to the end of this river ride as soon as possible.

Despite everything, I relaxed and enjoyed the ride.

CHAPTER 22

Gabe carried me out of the river at a waterfront park. We reached the west shore of the Willamette just south of the Hawthorne Bridge. As soon as I could, I let go and walked on my own. Water streamed from my clothes and hair, forming tiny spirals as it returned to the river.

"I can pull the water off your skin," Gabe said as he helped me keep my balance, "but I don't like to. I worry about accidentally sucking water out through someone's skin."

"That sounds bad."

"It is bad."

We scrambled up the rocky shore to a paved path. No one had seen us, or no one cared about two teenagers walking out of the river. Cars drove past on the nearby bridge and street. Ahead, I noted a couple strolling, their attention on each other. A brown-skinned man wearing swim trunks lay on a towel on the grass, sunbathing on New Year's Day. Another guy, this one in a light jacket and a kilt, rode a unicycle down the path while juggling bowling pins.

Portland, go figure.

"Why here?" I asked.

He waved for me to follow and jogged toward the sunbather. I followed at a more sedate walk, not sure I understood the point. So far, Gabe hadn't steered me wrong, of course. This didn't seem useful, though.

Gabe paused and beckoned for me to hurry up. "C'mon, Sophie. He won't bite."

I hadn't thought he would until Gabe said that. "But what will he do?"

We reached the man. Gabe leaned over him so the man could see him. "Hi, Dad."

Oh. Of course. Who else would sunbathe in January except for someone who embodied the cold of a river fed by melting snow?

The sunbather opened his eyes and grinned in an eerie echo of Gabe. "Gabriel! What are you doing here?" He jumped to his feet and hugged Gabe. "I didn't expect to see you again until summer." The river god saw me and brightened. "Who's this?"

"Sophie, this is Wimahl, my father. Dad, this is Sophie, my friend who needs help."

"A witch who wants help from a washed up river god, eh?" He smiled with friendly welcome and offered me his hand to shake.

I didn't want to be rude, so I shook it. "It's nice to meet you."

"Interesting. You're...huh. Shallow well but twisted like a corkscrew. Who taught you how to use your power, girl?"

Taken aback, I blinked and failed to form coherent words.

Gabe shrugged. "Her mom. She's like my mom, only worse."

Wimahl rolled his eyes. "White women. My people aren't so weird about things that don't fit their expectations." He jabbed a finger at me. "You're doing it all wrong."

I blushed. Hard. And still couldn't come up with anything to say.

"We have a problem," Gabe said.

"I can see that." Wimahl waved for us to sit. He and Gabe dropped to the towel with identical boneless grace.

Not sure how I felt about being considered a problem, I sat with less enthusiasm and speed. Then again, everyone had considered me a problem until Drew, so maybe I did know how I felt about it. I hated it.

"She's not the problem," Gabe said. "Another friend of ours is in danger, and we have to get something from Mom to save him. I was hoping you could help us find a way to get to Tigard fast."

"Is this other friend your boyfriend?"

"No."

"Ah, a true friend." Wimahl pulled a set of keys out of nowhere and tossed them at Gabe. "Take my car. But I can't let you go off to face danger without helping Sophie here."

Gabe snatched the keys out of the air. "We only have about four hours to sneak something out from under Mom's nose and get up to Sandy River."

"Traffic shouldn't be bad at this time of day. Bring the car straight back here and ride the river to the park. That'll take maybe an hour, plus a half hour to snooker your mom. Pad it with an extra half hour for good measure. That gives me two hours to teach Sophie how to use her power so she's not tying herself in knots every time she tries to do something."

I didn't understand what he meant, and I didn't like him. Trying not to annoy the river god in arm's reach, I said, "Please stop talking about me like I'm not here."

Wimahl blinked, then he covered his heart with his hands and bowed his head. "Pardon me. You're right. Gabriel introduced you as his friend, and I'm being far too familiar with you as a result." He sounded sincere, and I appreciated that. "May I have your permission to use some of your precious time to pursue a goal that will help my son, and therefore also you and your other friend, survive longer? I ask only for your attention and willingness to learn in unusual ways."

If a river god had something to teach me about using magic, I supposed I could give him a chance. After all, I'd reached the point of flying blind, grasping for anything to get through this nightmare. Besides, Drew would take Wimahl's offer without a second thought.

"We can probably afford a little time."

"You're very worried for this other friend." Wimahl nodded. "Is this the one you have the other links to?"

Of course he could see my aura in as much detail as Mom. Obviously he'd know everything without making an effort.

I nodded.

Wimahl held out his hand, palm up. Touching him seemed dangerous. I hesitated.

"You're a smart girl. Always stop and consider the risks when opening yourself to a strange entity. What is my motivation, you must wonder? I care about Gabriel. I'm sure this seems strange to you. I'll live forever. Why should I care about one child I'll have to watch die no matter what?"

The thought had flickered through my mind. He'd probably heard the question plenty of times.

He smiled at me and patted Gabe on the shoulder. "Gabriel is part of me. His power is my power. The water in his body is the water in my body. Rivers flow through me, and they flow through him. If something matters to him, it matters to me. That being the case, let me help you, please. Because someone has taught you very some wrong things."

For four years, I'd nursed a tiny, buried fantasy that one day, I'd discover I had more power than the entire coven put together, they'd just prevented me from accessing somehow. Wimahl hadn't offered that kind of revelation, of course. I knew that. Still...

"Can you explain what you mean first? I believe you, but I don't understand."

Wimahl smiled with approval, which warmed my heart. "Magic flows like water. You know this, I'm sure. You can see it. Living things generate it, the tiny spots roll together, and thus we get ley lines and nodes. Incidentally, I'm interested in discussing the node's awakening, but we can talk about that another time. But, like water. You've been taught to control it as if you could hold it in your hands and make it bend to your will."

Clear water coalesced above Wimahl's hand in a perfect sphere. "Tell me, can you hold water?" He offered the sphere to me.

Willing to play along, I held out my hands, cupping them. He turned his hand over to pour the sphere into them. The sphere fell apart and the water splashed on my skin and clothes.

"You see? Magic works the same, especially for someone of your type." He called the water to his hand, pulling it out of my clothing and off of my skin. "They see your shallow well and think you're useless, powerless, but you're not. Your power cannot spray water like theirs. They all have pipes, conduits. Like a firehose. Your power, the shallow well, is a plate. Not meant to spray. It's meant to shape. To create intricacy and intimacy. No wonder you've bound Gabriel and this other one to you, because what else could you do? It's what you were made for."

He offered me his hand again.

I blinked at him, trying to comprehend what he wanted to give. An end to four years of pain sounded too good to be true.

If I learned what he had to teach, would my mother love me again?

No, she would've had to love me in the first place. She'd never loved me. The kind of disappointment she'd shown didn't come from love. That came from ownership. Mom had thought of me as her possession, something that didn't perform as advertised. If she could've returned me to some store for a refund or exchange, she would have.

Tears rolling down my cheeks, I set my hand in his. "Please help me."

CHAPTER 23

I touched Wimahl and my vision faded to white. When it cleared, we stood in front of my parents' house in weak yellow light. Not my house. Not the real house, either. This one had no snow and no broken window.

The roses and trees had lost their leaves without gaining the gray of winter hibernation. Shriveled brown leaves littered the ground. Paint hung in ragged peels from the walls. Instead of standing upright, the juniper at the corner, the one I'd used to escape, hung limp with mottled brown needles.

This version of the house smelled wrong. I didn't often notice the scent of the front yard, and I couldn't say what counted as normal. Rot and brimstone, though, wasn't right. Likewise, the windows had a strange oily sheen and grimy crust.

Turning on the spot, I had no idea why Wimahl would bring me here. "Where are we?"

"I think you modern witches call it the outer sanctum. Through that door is your private sanctum. This part is a manifestation of where you meet another practitioner when you link auras temporarily. As far as I know, you'd only normally see this when you wind up in a metaphysical duel. This is where the enemy witch is when they attack."

I blinked at him. "This is me?"

"Yes." Wimahl crossed his arms and frowned at the scenery.

Why did my outer sanctum look like a creepy, abandoned house from a horror movie?

He crouched and prodded the wilted grass beneath our feet. "It needs more work than I expected."

"Wait. My inner sanctum is someplace else."

"That's not surprising. You clearly don't have a positive view of this place. Is this where your mother lives?"

"Yeah." I touched the nearest rose with a fingertip. The cane shed brownish spots like it had a virulent blight. "Is that why it's so terrible here?"

"Some of this is normal, especially at your age." He rapped his knuckles against the concrete of the front walk. A crack formed and ran across the surface to the edges. "The extent of it isn't. This outer sanctum reflects your usual baseline. How you feel most of the time. It doesn't change fast enough to show the peaks and valleys, just the basic landscape of you."

He stood and regarded me, stroking his chin. "From this, I'd expect you to suffer from suicidal depression. I've only just met you, but I think that's not the case?"

Though I'd entertained it earlier, I recoiled from the idea. "No, I don't want to die. I just want..." Something. Nothing felt right to fill that hole.

Wimahl nodded. "This is a monument to wrongness. You know how people talk about what matters is how you look on the inside? You're a pretty girl, and you know how to smile, how to keep yourself tidy and pleasant. But inside, you're dying."

My cheeks flared pink. I didn't want to believe him. "But I've changed things. I left home and found new friends. I don't want to go back."

"You're lying to yourself, Sophie." He smiled, soft and sad. "You crave this so hard it's killing you."

"No, I don't!" I covered my face. Hadn't I made a firm decision to never return? Why did Mom get to mess me up so much?

Wrapping his arms around me, Wimahl hummed a tune I didn't know. He stood and held me close. I listened to his heart beating and hated how much Mom made me cry. She didn't deserve all the tears I'd shed for her.

"There's no shame here. The heart wants what it wants, and we can only try to teach it why it's wrong. Tell me your most fervent wish. If you could have one thing, what would it be?"

My stupid mouth opened and said something stupid. "I want her to love me. Why won't she love me for who I am?"

Wimahl clucked his tongue. "Yes, that makes sense. Maybe someday she will. But not today. You can't make her see you as a person. She has to come to that on her own. I don't know her, so I have no advice for what that will take. You, on the other hand, need to recognize the hurt she's still causing even though you've cut her out of your life."

I sniffled. "And that will make my magic work better?"

"No." He pulled back with half a smile. "And yes. Think of your mother's influence like a poison that builds up over time. It weakens everything. Once you leave, your system begins to recover. Bit by bit, it flushes out the toxins. Step by step. Your magic will strengthen because your everything will strengthen.

"But this has nothing to do with how you use power. This is like brushing your teeth. How you use your power is more about which toothbrush you use. Sort of. It's not the best metaphor."

No one ever cared about how I felt or what I wanted.

That was a lie. Claire cared. So did Drew and Gabe. Claire's family cared too. None of them understood all this stuff, though, so Wimahl, my newest friend's dad, a river god, counted as the first person to worry about my mental health.

After we rescued Drew and escaped my mom, I'd return and talk to Wimahl more. He had important things to say, and I thought I needed to hear them. Right now, we didn't have time for me to get my head on straight.

"How do I pick a better toothbrush?"

Wimahl nodded his approval and let go of me. "Let's go inside."

Wiping my face, I smiled at the flicker of pride and hope in my chest. I opened the front door and found the interior of Claire's cabin. As before, the wood seemed gray and brittle, and all the leaves were dead and brown.

Touching a leaf made it crumble to flakes. "When I've had a chance to heal, will all this come alive?"

"Maybe not all of it, but a good amount, yes." He closed the door and examined the broken lock. Without a word, he left it to crouch and peer under the bed. "Here we go. Part of you knows you're using the power wrong, so you've hidden the channel where you can't see it."

He reached under the bed and removed a twisted mass of blue glass and metal as long and wide as his arm. "This is a complicated mess, isn't it?"

"What even is that?" How did he know I hid something under my bed when I didn't know that?

"It's a representation of your well of power. Every time you use magic, it has to flow through this thing. Think of it like an internal focus stone. If you want to keep with the toothbrushing metaphor, this is your teeth."

I stared at the ugly mass and had no idea what to do about it. No wonder everything took so much effort. To get from one end to the other, the power had to follow so many twists and turns it would sputter and die before ever reaching the end. "How did it get like that?"

"Years of using the power in ways you were never intended to use it. Your channels are adaptable to a certain degree. Every time you used the wrong toothbrush, you forced your teeth into a shape that didn't work for you. To put it another way, your power started with a small stream. The way you were taught to use it carved its path. For most witches, more water would flow into that path, attracted by the slope. For you, things work differently, so you wound up with this."

Apparently, I could hate my mom even more than I already did. I'd thought she only twisted my stomach into knots. Nope, she'd affected my whole being, inside and out.

Turning over the ugly thing in his hands, he frowned at it, then he shrugged. "I think I can teach you to unsnarl this, but that would take most of the rest of your life. May I have your permission to just fix it? I could do it without asking, but I've noticed humans appreciate the opportunity to refuse. Especially female ones."

It sounded like a trick question. Either I could spend years trying to bang the thing back into shape, fighting and struggling the whole way, or he could snap his fingers and make it right? "Yes, please?"

Wimahl raised his arms and my vision faded to blue. Coolness embraced and buoyed me. I saw nothing, but I tasted crisp clarity. Purity filled my nose. Silence wrapped me in a blanket. Stillness bubbled past my ears. Winter chilled me to the bone and heated my blood. My mouth opened and nothing came out.

I blinked several times. Finally, I saw the sky. Gabe sat over me, and I discovered he'd pulled my head into his lap. Wimahl held my hand.

Nothing felt different, except everything felt different. The blue sky looked bluer. Gabe's dark eyes held more depth. His dark hair gleamed with subtle brown highlights I hadn't noticed before.

The biggest thing? I could see his aura without trying. Blue rippled around him like flowing water. Wimahl leaned into view. His faint aura, a deeper blue than Gabe's, stuck close to his body and flickered as if it didn't want me to see.

"Much better." Wimahl laid my hand on my belly and patted it. "That will help a great deal, I think. Whoever taught you the basics was, to be plain, an idiot, and I would love to meet them so I can tell them so."

I couldn't find words. Mouth noises seemed so vulgar and pale compared to all the vibrant colors.

They talked. I gaped in awe at the world. And I cried, because of course I did.

CHAPTER 24

Wimahl offered me a handkerchief. He and Gabe helped me sit up. I wiped my face and fingered the damp square of folded cloth. All the stuff bouncing in my head seemed too stupid to say out loud, so I said nothing.

"Let's talk a little bit about how you're going to use your magic to not get Gabriel killed." Wimahl patted my knee. His touch through my jeans reminded me of a cool drink on a warm summer day. "If we had plenty of time, I'd give you some exercises to work on and ask you to come back tomorrow, and the next day, and keep coming back until you feel competent. Since we can't do that right now, and you need some basics, I'm going to do what I can and ask you to come back when you have a chance."

I nodded and wiped my nose again. "Will any of it hurt?"

He cocked his head and blinked at me. "No, of course not. If it hurts, we're doing it wrong."

Screw you, Mom. "Okay."

Taking my hand, Wimahl gave me an encouraging smile. "The important thing is not to force it. The way power flows is the way you use it."

"I was told I have an affinity for water."

He snorted. "In a crude way, this is true, but it misses the point. All magic behaves like water. Everyone who uses it has an affinity for that. Otherwise, you wouldn't be able to use it. Some traditions of witches believe in this affinity nonsense. It's a way of thinking about magic, not a way of using it. A construct to wrap your mind around. It's your worldview, your temperament, your attitudes, and your beliefs that shape how you use the power."

As much as he sounded like a hokey New Age practitioner, I listened. My heart yearned for a different explanation than Mom and the coven had given me. Those women had lied to me so much. Wimahl threw me a lifeline when all I could figure out was drowning.

"This all sounds well and good, but what does it mean? It means that magic can do anything if you want it hard enough. Except." He raised a finger. "It cannot make something out of nothing. Matter cannot be created, only changed from one state to another. This principle of physics applies to magic. We can change things quite a bit more than just liquid to solid or gas, but the idea is the same.

"Likewise, power doesn't disappear when we use it. As with water, all the power that has ever existed still exists. It ebbs and flows. It changes state. It moves from one place to another. When we use it, the power isn't expended. Whatever we've done with it, that energy moves or changes state. It might be dispersed to rejoin the system, or it might get stored in an object like your coat."

So far, this all seemed simple. Why had the coven given me so many boundaries? To control me? Did they fear me for some reason? No, that didn't make sense. Or did it?

"And the other exception? Magic cannot directly change what a person thinks or feels. It can, however, insert insidious thoughts and feelings into the mind. The larger and more dissonant the inserted thought, the more likely your mind is to reject it. If I magically compel you to hate pizza, you can shrug it off. If I magically compel you to think of yourself as getting fat from eating pizza, you're more likely to accept it and avoid pizza."

I knew some girls at school who would beg for a diet plan like that. The idea of getting them to pay me for what boiled down to magical behavior modification made me smirk.

"It's worth mentioning that magic can, to a certain extent, create life. It can increase intelligence to the point of sentience. It can turn birds into dragons and horses into unicorns. It can also change people into monsters. As, I think, you already know."

Yes, I did know that.

"It doesn't surprise me you were given more limits. This is common. I have specific, peculiar limits because I have a specific, peculiar area of influence. We gods cannot do anything we want at any time, in any way. We're constrained in more ways than one. Witches, though, have self-imposed limitations."

I blinked at him. "Why?"

Wimahl shrugged. "Because men fear them. Over and over throughout history, women trying to make things better have roused the wrath of men who like things the way they are. I've never understood it myself. But I've seen it. The tribes I served didn't understand it either, which is how the white men managed to overwhelm us. It didn't help that much of my power is locked in a box elsewhere, but that's another story for another day."

"But..." I still didn't quite understand. "Witches can do literally anything with magic, but we don't let ourselves? How does that work? I mean, why would my grandmother have taught my mom those limitations?"

"The limitations grew out of need, and those needs surfaced hundreds of years ago. Think of the Church's Inquisition. Men with enough power to defeat witches hunted and killed them with special tools for that purpose. Under that kind of threat, wouldn't you stop doing anything that called attention to yourself? And then teach your daughters the same concerns?"

I wanted to disagree. I wanted to say no, I'd rise up with Claire, Drew, and Gabe, and anyone else we knew to stop the Inquisition. But I knew the real answer. Survival was the real answer. Like anyone else, I'd do what it took to survive. I'd hide if the threat scared me, or if that would save other lives.

"Now you see. Now you understand. This time, when magic is revealed again, is a dangerous difficult time for all of us. We face threats we haven't faced in over a millennium. Not long ago, giant bugs swelled by magic attacked the city. In other places, other things will happen. Fear will drive people to hate all of us again. This moment is a time to discover who is your ally and who is your enemy, and it's a time to practice the skills you'll need in the coming months and years."

A war had begun and no one realized it yet. By the time people figured it out, we needed to be ready. I'd never thought of myself as a soldier before.

"What do we do?" I don't know why I whispered.

"For the moment, save your friend. Our relationships are important. Beyond that, you're about to discover the paralysis of limitless options. Here is how you use magic as a witch who knows the truth. Don't focus on what you see or how it appears to work. Focus on the magic itself. Change its state. Disperse it. Bring it together. Take from here to deprive there. Think in simple, basic terms."

I thought I understood the idea. Probably. Going to face adult witches without time to practice this new way of thinking seemed dumb. No, it didn't. It scared me.

"When I build a shield, what am I really doing?"

"What do you think you're doing?"

"Dad," Gabe said, chiding him. I'd almost forgotten he sat beside me.

"No, he's right." I rubbed my cheeks, trying to come up with the words to explain. "I think I'm shoving power between me and an attack."

Wimahl waved off Gabe. "Knowing what you now know, what's your real answer?"

Frowning, I tried to render my actions to simple terms. What lay at the core of how it worked? "I'm changing the magical power of my aura from…a gas to a solid? And taking from there to here?"

He beamed at me. "Yes. Good. Think more about this on your drive to Tigard. Deconstruct actions you know how to do already."

Using magic boiled down to four acts—change, disperse, collect, steal. The simplicity left me breathless. All this time, I'd thought it had to nurture or grow. That it only affected plants and pests.

Gabe took my hand and helped me stand. "Thanks, Dad. I'll have the car back before dark for sure."

Wimahl nodded. "Good luck. I hope to see you again soon. And your friend."

"Me too." I waved as I followed Gabe to the parking lot beyond the grass and trees. A whole new world lay before me. Time to get some stuff done and figure out what my mom wanted before she killed somebody.

Please let Drew be okay.

CHAPTER 25

Wimahl owned a silver Porsche. For the drive to Tigard, I sat in the passenger seat, oblivious to the view out the windows. Every fiber of my being ran through every single thing I'd done with magic in the past few months, analyzing and dissecting each.

Force-growing plants? Change and collect. Blocking power blasts? Disperse. Recharging after exhausting myself? Steal. Shattering Drew's aura and awakening his witch powers? Disperse and change.

I knew how to do all four of the actions. Which meant I could do anything. Wait, no. How could I fix a broken body? Did it work like force-growing a plant? Did that make sense? "How did you and Drew heal me?"

Gabe shrugged. "Water is inherently soothing and life-giving. I encased you in a glob of water from the faucet, and Drew triggered a metaphysical something-or-other. He didn't really pause to explain his part. We were kind of pressed for time what with you dying and all."

"He stole from you to do what he did." For a moment, that answered the question. Then I frowned. "Why would he need to steal from you? He has the node to draw from, and he's practically a firehose for power."

"Maybe he didn't so much need the power as the direction? I mean, he said straight-up that he's a battery. I don't think he has much ability to control the power he can access."

Yes, that sounded right. Did he have the capacity to learn from

Wimahl like I did? Maybe the way we'd blasted him wide open had insured he needed help. I'd accidentally created a partner and bound myself to him. Individually, neither of us could do a whole lot. Together, we could truly do anything.

"If Mom figures out how we work together, she'll be terrified of us."

Drew had taken my tokens and kept them. If Mom managed to break into his private sanctum, she'd break our bindings. We'd both be screwed. No, all three of us. Gabe needed us too. Drew had bindings to Claire and the node too. He practically served as a node of sorts for everyone he cared about.

"We're going as fast as we can, Sophie. You can't sit there and worry about every possibility for something to go wrong. You'll paralyze yourself with fear. Stay on task. Right now, we need to get that key from my mom."

"Can I panic about how to do that instead?"

He chuckled. "I'm pretty sure both she and my other dad are home right now. They're probably even wondering where I am since I said I was going to see you, and that was—" He checked the clock in the car dashboard. "—six hours ago. We still have three hours left, and we're almost there, so we should have plenty of time to roll with whatever we find at my house."

If he'd left home six hours ago, I'd fled my house about five hours ago. Everything I'd dealt with today, including almost dying twice, had happened in such a short amount of time. In three more hours, at five o'clock, we'd meet my mom in the woods near a giant rosebush and save Drew's life.

The meet would happen after sunset, in the dim gloom of a clear-sky twilight. Ugh. No, think about dealing with Gabe's mom and finding that key.

"Do you think your mom moved the key or not?"

"No idea."

"Do you have a plan?"

Gabe nodded. "We're going to walk in through the front door and pretend we're a couple. We'll go upstairs, pretending to go to my room to make out, and go to hers instead."

I stared at him. "We're going to use making out as a cover story for searching her room and stealing her key?"

He shrugged. "She wants me to seduce you."

"If I'd ever tried to bring a boy, any boy, to my room and close the door, I would've gotten knocked on my ass and grounded so fast it'd make your head spin."

"You're a girl."

Right. He had a point. "Okay. I guess if that'll work, I have no problem with it. We'll have to act like that's something we want to do, though. No offense, but that's a stretch. I mean, I'm happy to touch you, but I'm really more interested in Claire."

I froze. I'd intended to say Drew, but I'd said Claire.

Gabe glanced at me with a bemused smile and a raised brow. "I knew it."

My cheeks burned hard. "What?"

"I could tell from the way you said her name and when you called her Drew's girlfriend. You practically glow when you mention her."

Unable to come up with a response, I snapped my mouth shut.

"Come on, Sophie. If anyone can figure out who's a repressed bisexual, or whatever, it's a guy who's forced to live in the closet."

Hunching on myself, I crossed my arms and glared at the floor. Bisexuals did all kinds of weird, crazy things, or so I'd heard. "I'm not."

"Sure. You keep telling yourself that. I'll be over here, ready to gloat when you realize I'm right."

"Jerk."

He laughed, the jerk. "I'm not going to out you. That's your business. If you want to pretend like you only want Drew, go ahead and keep on pretending. Besides, he's cute. Red hair, freckles, glasses, and a nerd." Gabe sighed wistfully. "So inoffensive. Wants to please everyone. Just enough of a take-charge attitude without being overbearing. If he was gay, I'd be all over that. But no one's perfect."

I laughed, which annoyed me, and that made me cry.

"Poor Sophie. Too many things are happening to you too fast. You need some time to decompress and we don't have any." He pointed forward. "That's my house."

Wiping my face with Wimahl's handkerchief, I followed his finger. His house looked a lot like my parents' house. Tidy, winterized gardens and leafless trees surrounded a two-story home in a tasteful pale yellow with white trim. A thin, faint green aura surrounded it. Aside from the aura, which no regular person would ever see, the house fit with its neighbors in exactly the same way every other witch's house I'd ever seen did.

When Wimahl had mentioned not calling attention to ourselves, I hadn't realized he'd meant in every aspect of our lives. We all met the expectations of our neighborhoods. Thinking about it more, I realized witches with jobs didn't excel and climb the management ladder, they did their work with enough competence to stay employed. At school, we all did well enough to get into college without rising to the top of the class.

Mom had interrupted my homework on more than one occasion for witch things. When I'd complained about the impact on my grades, she'd always said I did well enough. My brothers, on the other hand, both got harassed and hounded to finish their homework, do it right, study for the test, scrape the extra credit, go above and beyond, play sports as hard as they could, and reach for the stars.

Even Ashley, who got the attention of a pretty girl, didn't put as much effort into her looks as other girls did. She didn't try to snare the best boyfriend. In fact, she'd dated a string of average guys, always in our own grade. With some makeup and the right clothes, I knew she could catch the attention of our school's quarterback or the top brains in the senior class. But she never tried.

Witches blended. Boys excelled.

I hated my mom, I hated the coven, and I hated everything I'd learned from those women. They'd taught us to aspire to mediocrity on purpose. Don't stand out. Don't strive. Don't try. Everything for the coven. Devote yourself to growing roses because nothing else matters. Wallow in lies.

Kill your dreams.

I didn't even have any dreams anymore. What would I hope for? One less disappointed look per day? A lifetime of tending rosebushes?

To hell with that. I wanted something special. No matter the cost, I'd find a way to make a difference for someone.

CHAPTER 26

Gabe shut off the engine in the driveway. He hustled around the car to open the door for me in case anyone watched. I forced myself to smile like I wanted him. Pretending Claire offered me her arm helped. She didn't smell like the Willamette, but she did have strong arms, and she did stand several inches taller than me.

I couldn't muster a giggle, but I could keep smiling. Gabe took my hand and opened the door. We stepped inside. The house's aura pressed against me, which felt like walking into plastic wrap. Unlike Mom's warding, this didn't constrain me. It struck me as more of a warning system than a protection system.

An attractive woman with dark hair and pearls sat in the room to the left. Her aura glimmered green. She stopped tapping on a laptop to look up at us.

"Hi, Mom." Gabe had her nose. With his tanned complexion, he looked a lot more like his dad.

She smiled with welcome. "Who's this?" As if she didn't know.

"Oh, right. Sorry." He sounded like he'd genuinely forgotten he needed to introduce us. "Mom, this is my girlfriend, Sophie Harris. Sophie, this is my mom, Lana Avenatti."

Sticking by Gabe's side, I beamed at her. "It's nice to meet you, Mrs. Avenatti."

"How lovely." Mrs. Avenatti radiated warm approval. "Would you like something to drink?"

"Nah, we're just going up to my room for a while." Gabe tugged me toward the carpeted stairs. He grinned like he had a dirty secret.

"Good." Mrs. Avenatti returned her attention to her laptop. "Your brother is out with his friends, so you won't bother him. Will you be staying for dinner, Sophie?"

"I don't think so?" I checked with Gabe as if I couldn't make a decision like that for myself.

"Probably not. I mean, we have school tomorrow, and I'll have to take her home." He nudged me up the stairs and smacked my ass.

I squealed. Then I wrangled it into a giggle.

"Okay. Let me know if you change your mind. Have fun."

Halfway up the stairs, I couldn't see her anymore. If we'd acted like that in front of my mom, she wouldn't have smiled. She would've followed us upstairs and into my room, then asked pointed questions about our plans for the afternoon. Not until she thought she'd made herself clear that she wouldn't tolerate any handsiness from Gabe would she have left us alone. Even then, she would've required my door to stay open.

But Gabe's mom practically told us to get naked together. And that made sense somehow.

Whatever. I rushed the rest of the way up the stairs. Glancing behind me, I saw Gabe point at the closed door at the end of the hall.

Letting out another burst of giggles, I hit the door and opened it. Someone else lay on the king size bed, reading a book. The man had short, dark hair shot through with gray, and wore sweats with thick, fuzzy socks.

I froze. My cheeks flared with a light blush. Gabe ran into me. He laughed and wrapped his arms around me.

"Sorry, Dad." Gabe picked me up and kissed my neck. "This is my parents' room. Mine is that other door."

Raising both hands to cover my mouth, I opened my eyes as wide as they could go. "Oh, my gosh! I'm so sorry!"

Mr. Avenatti rolled his eyes and sighed. "Keep the noise down, Gabe. And close the door."

"You heard him." He set me on my feet again and rubbed his nose against mine. As he pulled the door shut, he said, "No screaming."

I blushed so hard my head hurt. Then I smacked his arm. "I can't believe you said that," I whispered.

He snorted and opened his bedroom door. We fled inside and shut the door. Gabe lived in an ocean of blue. His room had gray carpet, but everything else was the color of the Willamette on a good day. Nothing sat out, as if he'd made an effort to clean his room before leaving this morning. Even my tidy room had more mess than this.

"Now what?"

"I'm not sure. I thought he'd be downstairs, watching TV."

I took a deep breath. "I'm not going to panic."

"Neither am I." Gabe paced across the floor, rubbing his forehead. "Okay. If you have to find an enchanted object, how do you do that? Say it's in a pile of stuff in plain sight and you're not sure which thing to grab."

"Focus so I can see magical auras, then paw through all of it." Not that I had to focus anymore to see auras. Ley lines still didn't show up, though, so maybe I had to focus to see anything weak or blocked from immediate view.

"Can you see something like that through a wall?"

"Yesterday, I would've said no. Today, I'm going to just try it. Go stand in the hallway to give me a control to work with."

"I'll stand in the bathroom across the hall." He left the room, taking care to make as little noise as possible with the door.

"Okay." My turn to pace. I stalked across Gabe's room and returned, remembering every word Wimahl had said. Detecting magic didn't take changing, collecting, dispersing, or stealing. Or did it? Would I see things easier and clearer if I thought about it in one of those ways?

Thinking through the options, collecting seemed the best choice. If I could get magic to collect around the house, I could check all the places where it formed globs or pools, or whatever the right term was. Could I do that through walls? Only one way to find out.

I closed my eyes and raised my arms like a conductor calling for attention. The magic would dance to my music. This would work.

Pulling on my connection to Drew, I reached for anything I could find nearby. There, power collected around Gabe. Farther away, small eddies swirled in different parts of the house. At least, I thought they all existed inside the building. Without knowing the full layout, I couldn't say for sure.

Then I noticed a larger pool below me. This swirl grew with every passing moment. Crap, I hadn't considered how the power would collect around Gabe's mom. If she noticed me messing with magic in her house...

My mom didn't like strange witches existing inside her house, let alone doing anything. Gabe's mom thought I still belonged to Petal Society, so she'd see the target of her machinations turning the tables on her.

In a panic, I tried to reel back the magic like a fishing line. That didn't work. It kept spinning to the side, then returning to Gabe's mom. She magnetically attracted it. I backed against the wall, frantically trying to cut it off. Why wouldn't it stop?

Gabe's Mom burst through the door. "What are you doing in my house?" she bellowed.

Seeing her and freezing in terror snapped the feeding tube I'd inadvertently set up between us. Power stopped flowing.

"I'm sorry," I whimpered. "I was just..." Doing what? Looking for something to steal from her wouldn't fly. I had nothing to offer that wouldn't sound terrible.

"You were just spying for the Petal Society!"

"Whoa, Mom, wait." Gabe tried to shove her aside.

She stood firm, her power rooting her to the spot. A bulldozer couldn't have moved her. "I knew it was too good to be true." Her aura flared, and she snatched Gabe's wrist.

This five-foot-three, slim woman wearing pearls and ballet flats wrenched around the six-foot hotshot soccer player and slammed him against the wall in the hallway with his hand twisted behind his back.

Gabe groaned. I blinked. Then I did something stupid. I flung power at her, this time to disperse instead of collect. Before she noticed, I rushed her. My body slammed into hers. The three of us landed in a heap on the carpet.

I jabbed Mrs. Avenatti with an elbow. Gabe wriggled and squirmed. His mom growled and kicked.

Fine. If she wanted a magically enhanced wrestling match, she'd get a magically enhanced wrestling match. I slapped my hand on her shoulder. Though Drew's power didn't feed me, I could still steal hers. At least, I thought I could. So I tried. Mrs. Avenatti's power siphoned through my hands and disappeared. I had no idea where it went, other than not back to her.

Gabe reached toward me. I took his hand. We hadn't tried to use our power together, but I had no doubt it would work. Drew and I had figured things out on the fly. Gabe and I could too.

The moment I'd half-dreaded happened. My vision blanked for a moment, then I stood in the middle of a barren winter forest under overcast skies. Brown, dead leaves huddled in clusters at the bases of dark, empty tree trunks. Shrubs thick with thorns leaned toward me. The ground was one big, swampy mud pit.

The place had one bright spot. Gabe stood at my back, holding my hand.

We could do this if we worked together.

CHAPTER 27

Gabe squeezed my hand. "Where are we? What's going on?" I felt him shifting to check in every direction.

"This is a metaphysical space. I don't know if we're here physically or not, but probably not. I forced your mom into a sort of a duel." By accident, but I didn't want to tell him that in case it made him falter. "We don't have to beat her, but we do have to find her and not let her beat us."

"Sure." He snorted. I could relate. "No problem. You lead, because I've got no idea."

"Can you manipulate the water in the mud?"

He paused for a moment, then a globe of water coalesced in the air. "Yes. Does that mean we're physically here?"

"I'm not sure. But let's go with yes. Your job is to do whatever you can to neutralize your mom while I try to get information." Nothing suggested a direction, which meant it didn't matter which way we tried. "Think really hard about wanting to confront your mom."

"I don't want to confront my mom."

"I know. Neither do I. But we have to if we want that key." For once, I squeezed his hand. "C'mon. The sooner we find her, the sooner we can get out of here."

I picked a direction and tugged on his hand. Find Lana Avenatti. Find Lana Avenatti. Find Lana Avenatti. My feet squelched in the mud to the rhythm of those words repeating in my head. Nothing else mattered.

Within minutes, we reached a round cabin in the woods with a closed door and light glowing in the single window.

Wait. I didn't want to break into Lana Avenatti's private sanctum. We needed information, not domination. I wanted to take a key she owned and nothing more.

A dozen feet from the door, I stopped.

Gabe bumped into me. "What's wrong? Is this where to find her?"

"Yes. I'm just not sure this is what we really want. If we beat down that door, we're no better than my mom. We're no better than any of the witches in either coven."

Gabe frowned. "I hate how she treats me. I can't be myself because of her. She wants me to fit into a neat little box she's made up, and I don't. I just don't. That perfect son she wants isn't me. Maybe some other guy would be happy like that, but I can't be."

I understood. His mom problems and my mom problems had a lot in common. For roses. All of this crap they put us through won them stupid prizes for stupid flowers. So many people had become obsessed with this stupid war for no reason.

Patting his arm, I nodded toward the cabin. "Why don't you try talking to her through the door? This doesn't have to be a fight."

He sighed and slumped his shoulders. "There's nothing I can do here. She's known how to counter me since I was a kid. I can't beat her. And I have nowhere else to go. She's my mom."

Gabe sounded like me before I'd grasped how thoroughly Claire and Drew would welcome me. "You can stay with us. With Drew and me. With Claire and her family. We won't turn you out."

"What if I don't get along with any of them?"

I smiled at him. "You get along with me. And I think Drew is okay with you. That just leaves Claire. Her family will take in anyone so long as you're willing to help with chores."

He answered my smile with a weak one of his own. "And you're in love with Claire, so you're pretty sure you can talk her into it."

Blushing, I looked at my feet. "I don't know how how I feel about her." I nudged him toward the door. "Just know you have someplace to go if you need it."

Nodding, he shuffled forward. "Mom? I guess you're in there, and I'm hoping you can hear me."

A shadow passed by the window.

"I never wanted to hurt you, Mom. I just— I'm tired of pretending to be someone I'm not. I'm gay. I've known it for a long time. And you've known it for a while too. Every time you tell me it doesn't matter, you're telling me that I don't matter. That who I am isn't as important as what you want. That you don't care."

Could I find a way to explain all this to my own mom? She'd done so much to me. I couldn't say it would matter if she listened while I poured out my pain.

"I feel like I should apologize for not being what you hoped for, but I won't. I'm not sorry for who I am. I'm not going to lie about it anymore either. If you can't handle that, then I guess I have nothing more to say to you. Not that we've talked about anything in a while."

Gabe laid his palm on the door and bowed his head. "I wish I could've been something more to you than a means to an end. I wish you could've seen me for one moment as your son instead of as a tool. I wish...I wish a lot of things. But I guess I'm done wishing because it's just flipping coins into a fountain and getting nothing in return."

He turned away from the door. My heart hurt for him.

The door cracked open. His mom poked her head through.

I held my breath. Whatever he chose, I'd be there for him.

Gabe didn't look back. He plodded to me, defeated and deflated. "Let's go."

How did we escape this scenario? I had no real idea. Instead of trying, though, I slid an arm around his waist to walk with him.

Between one step and another, we landed in the hallway. All three of us sat along one wall with me between Gabe and his mom. Mrs. Avenatti must have thrown us out.

The next time I could, I promised myself I'd practice using my magic. I'd experiment in every way I could. Drew and I would take the fundamentals Wimahl had taught me and build a fortress around us. And Gabe.

"What does the Petal Society want in my house?" she asked, sounding wary and weary.

"I renounced my coven membership a week ago."

She turned and regarded me like she'd never heard anything more unbelievable in her life. "Why?"

Screw you, lady. I didn't meet her gaze. "I met some people who taught me I deserve better. Just like Gabe does."

"Is that coven falling apart?"

Her son just told her he wanted to walk out of her life, and she asked about the coven? Extra double screw you, lady. I lurched to my feet and tugged on Gabe's hand. "You have a magical iron key. I want it. Give it to me or we'll force another duel and I won't hold back. With or without Gabe by my side, I will mess you up."

She narrowed her eyes. "So that's what this—"

Gabe slapped her, which made me start in surprise. "No. No more." Water streamed from the bathroom to cocoon her. "I'm done with your crap. I gave you a chance, and you can't think of anything but your stupid coven's feud with another stupid coven!" His voice rose steadily until he shouted at her. "I don't care about the Petal Society, I don't care about the Rose Quarter, and I don't care if Dad knows I'm not his son. I don't care if the whole world knows I'm gay!"

By this point, I had no intention of interrupting while he finished excising the poison in his veins. Water engulfed all of Mrs. Avenatti except her face and ears, keeping her from moving. Though I suspected she could control magic with that much of her flesh exposed, she didn't try. I kept power at the ready to shield Gabe anyway. The woman had given me no reason to trust her.

"Have you ever done anything for someone else in your whole life? Have you ever stopped for one moment to think about someone besides yourself? I will never understand how someone as polite and kind as my real father would ever have wanted anything to do with you. And I will never understand why that man," he pointed at the bedroom door, "agreed to marry you."

I noticed that the door stood half open. Mr. Avenatti, who must've heard the scuffle earlier, leaned against the wall with his head bowed, listening with a pained frown.

Mrs. Avenatti's nostrils flared. She said nothing. Like me, she probably couldn't think of anything to say that would improve the situation.

Gabe spat at her. The gob of saliva hit her nose, making her flinch. "Where's the key?"

She still said nothing.

"Gabe," his dad said in a weary, broken voice. "I didn't know."

Why did our moms do such terrible things while our dads bobbled along, unaware of the pain in their families? My father didn't deserve a pass for not noticing how mom treated me. Gabe's didn't get a cookie either.

"Of course you didn't," Gabe snapped.

As much as I wanted to let Gabe vent to his heart's content, we had a deadline. "Mr. Avenatti? Have you seen a set of iron keys, like the kind they used in medieval times? One of them would be about this big with a handle shaped kind of like a rose."

He nodded.

"Don't tell them," Mrs. Avenatti growled. "It's too dangerous."

Gabe glared at his mom. "Tell us or I'll drown her."

I couldn't tell if he meant it or not. Getting out of this with no one dead seemed impossible.

CHAPTER 28

"Gabriel Nicolo Avenatti," his mom snarled.

Water covered her mouth. Her eyes widened and she snapped her mouth shut.

"I'm not kidding." Gabe shifted his glare to his dad. "After everything she's done to me, I'm not messing around."

Did I intervene? Did I let it play out? Would this work? Did I want to deal with Gabe after he killed his mom? I covered my face but peeked through my fingers. If Gabe's dad didn't give in soon, I'd do something. Either way, we'd talk about it in the car. This situation made me feel so gross and helpless.

Mr. Avenatti's frown deepened. "I thought I raised you better than that."

"You did." Gabe jabbed a finger at his mom. "She didn't."

Gabe's dad glanced at his wife, his expression conflicted and pained. "That's your mother. How can you do that to your mother?"

"The same way she decided her precious coven mattered more than me! I'm deciding that my friends matter more than her."

His gaze on his wife, Gabe's dad sighed and nodded. "They're hanging in the kitchen as decorations. Next to the pantry."

Hiding something in plain sight sounded like a dangerous gamble. I did not, at that moment, care. I did care that we could've avoided this whole mess by me getting a glass of water before heading upstairs.

The water sloughed off Gabe's mom to splash the carpet. She fell over, coughing and gasping for air. Though he could have, Gabe didn't remove any of the water from her clothes or the rug.

"Don't worry about me coming back. I won't." Gabe took my hand.

We hopped over his mom and hurried down the stairs. I wondered what his parents would do. They could report him as a runaway. So could mine. Finishing high school would become a challenge for both of us. Once we rescued Drew, I supposed we could enroll anywhere we wanted and all go to the same school someplace far away.

Gabe led the way to the kitchen. Granite countertops, chrome appliances, track lighting, and hardwood floors created a bright, elegant space. The room seemed too clean to me, like no one used it for cooking. My dad had serious chef-worthy skills, and my mom liked to bake. They kept the kitchen clean, but it felt lived-in. Used. This one probably saw only take-out boxes and frozen dinners.

Such a waste to have so much kitchen and use it so little.

The moment Gabe took a step toward the pantry, I zeroed in on the key. It hung on the wall like his dad had said. Even if it didn't look the same as the other one had, its tiny pink aura stood out like a neon sign in the mundane room.

"There." I pointed.

Gabe rushed across the room and lifted the entire set of keys off the hook. "Let's get out of here."

He ran for the front door. I followed.

His mom stepped into our path from the stairs, still soaking wet. She gazed at him with cool indifference, the kind of frigid anger that usually caused me to wilt. "I can't let you take that. My grandmother entrusted it to me for safekeeping."

"I really don't care what you say." Gabe tossed the keys to me. The water dripping from his mom sprang from her. I saw the hate and anger in his snarl, and I knew what he intended to do.

I had to stop him.

Time slowed. I watched the keys fly toward me. The water hovered around Mrs. Avenatti, rippling in a shell half an inch from her body. Gabe held out one hand with his palm open, ready to clench it into a fist. With that simple gesture, he'd crush his mom from head to toe.

For a moment, maybe even as long as an hour, he'd revel in the power and righteousness of inflicting so much harm on someone who'd hurt him so much. Then the guilt would crash around him. Whether he killed her or not, he'd become the villain, and he'd realize it too late to change anything.

First, I snagged the keys out of the air. Then I kicked the back of Mrs. Avenatti's knee. Finally, I looped my arm through Gabe's and hauled him to the door. Time eased forward as I yanked open the door. As the world returned to full speed, I used our momentum to throw him to the ground, then whipped around and slammed the door shut.

"Let's go!"

Gabe blinked at me. He lay on his back on the brown grass beside the concrete of the front walk because I'm not a jerk. "What the—?"

I held up the keys. "We're out, we've got the keys, and your mom is coming. Let's go. Now!"

"But I just—"

The front door cracked open. He shut up and scrambled to his feet. I ran to the car. He'd left it unlocked, so I wrenched open my door and dove inside. Gabe did the same. His mom stepped through the door.

Actually, she limped. I'd kicked her knee pretty hard. Which she deserved. Death, no. Knee problems, yes.

Gripping the doorframe, she bared her teeth at us. Gabe stuck the key into the ignition. I wanted to slow time without affecting Gabe or the car, and I had no idea how to do that. Change? Disperse? Collect? Steal? Since I had no idea how I even affected time, I didn't know how to shape it.

Skip to the next idea, Sophie. Also, put on your seatbelt.

While Mrs. Avenatti flung power at us in an attack, I readied to take that power and shunt it down the line to wherever it could go. Stealing. As the power hit my funnel, Gabe started the engine. His mom smiled in grim satisfaction. The attack slid across my plate and kept going.

The car leaped out of the driveway. Mrs. Avenatti's smile faded. Gabe shifted through the gears like a pro racer. The attack stopped. We screamed down the street. I twisted to watch through the rear windshield.

She didn't jump on a broom to follow us. She didn't even shamble to the end of the driveway. The car kept going. We turned a corner, and I lost sight of the house.

Neither Gabe nor I said a word for at least five long minutes. In that time, I separated the key we needed from the rest and dropped the mundane ones on the floor.

"What did you do?"

I thought about playing dumb. The anger in his voice gave me pause. Gabe needed gentleness, not sarcasm.

"I stopped you from murdering your mom."

At a red light, he slammed on the brakes and seethed in silence. He opened his mouth once, then shut it, and then did it again. Another minute or two passed. The light changed. He drove on.

He let out a deep breath. "Thank you."

"You're welcome."

We still had two hours and forty-five minutes and only needed a half hour to reach the park. Why had mom picked four hours, anyway? That put us well into twilight, if not darkness among the trees. Her drive to the park shouldn't have taken more than an hour, and she would've known that from driving to Grandma Gert's in the first place.

Four hours seemed excessive if she wanted to keep us from thinking. Granted, she could've thought we'd have trouble reaching the key and the park without Drew to get us there. Considering our problems, though, it didn't sound like her. She'd picked that time for a reason that mattered to her.

"I really do hate her," Gabe said.

"I know," I said without thinking about it. "That's okay. You're not a bad person for hating her. I hate my mom too."

What would Mom want to do before we met to trade the key for Drew? Set up an ambush, probably. Or maybe she had something else in mind. Even though no one had said so, I knew she had to have asked Anne and Stace to send me after that first key. With her ability to read auras, she would've known more about the power sink hiding the key than I could ever have deciphered.

I replayed how the sink had affected me and thought about what might've happened without my link to Drew. Anne and Stace had claimed a more powerful witch would get burned out by the sink. Knowing now that no one in the coven had any problems lying to me about anything and everything, I had a sneaking suspicion they'd sent me to get the key knowing it would burn me out.

My former coven, made up of people who claimed me as blood, had sent me on purpose to burn out the witch powers I had that they considered pathetic and meager. For a reason.

"Gabe?"

"Yeah?"

"Let's go to my parents' house."

He glanced at me in surprise. "Why?"

"I want to read my mom's diary."

CHAPTER 29

Gabe stared out the front windshield for a few beats. We drove up I-5, heading into downtown Portland. If he wanted to return the car, he needed to take the next exit. "What if she's there?"

"Then we catch her off-guard while she's in the middle of prepping for us. If she's not, we could maybe go to the park now and catch her in the middle of setting up an ambush there, but we definitely won't learn anything about why that spot at that park with that rosebush. I'm feeling pretty confident that knowing will help us deal with her."

"Knowledge is power."

"Yeah."

He nodded. "Okay."

We didn't take the exit. Instead, he drove over the bridge, and we kept going. Companionable quiet settled between us, giving me too much room to think.

I thought about Drew. My mom hated him so much. She thought we'd slept together, and that had angered her in such a deep, visceral way. Like she'd needed a virgin sacrifice for some reason and Drew had ruined everything.

No, I didn't think anyone's sex life or the lack thereof mattered to magic. Ashley's abilities hadn't changed at all after she'd done it.

Mom's issues centered on control. She never wanted to let me choose or decide anything for myself. Going back home so soon had been a mistake, I now knew. Our relationship would've benefitted from me staying away for a month or more instead of just a week. Maybe a makeover like Sandra Dee had gotten in *Grease* would've helped.

If anything would've helped, that is.

Gabe parked on the street in front of my house. "Do you want me to come in with you or keep the car running so we have a quick escape?"

The wards on the house had always been visible to me. With my new capabilities, I could see details I'd never noticed before. For example, the surface swirled with a warning I'd never seen before that the wardings included lethal traps. Anyone with an active aura would trigger them.

I'd need to disable Mom's warding enough to get through without triggering anything or alerting her to my presence. Which I had no idea how to do but several thoughts on what to try.

Wimahl had done a lot more for me than teaching a simple lesson in how magic works. When we finished with all of this and I didn't have to worry about Mom anymore, I wanted to go down to that park and thank him. And also help his son settle in with Claire's family. Maybe help Gabe find a boyfriend too.

"Stay in the car. If you have to move it, meet me on the other side of the school." I pointed across the street.

"Are you sure?"

"I'm pretty sure I can only get myself safely through the wards."

"That's a good reason."

I leaned over and kissed his cheek, knowing he wouldn't take it the wrong way. Then I stepped out of the car and faced my parents' house, maybe for the last time.

If my mother forced me to, I would sever all ties. I didn't need Mom, Dad, my little brothers, or anyone in the Petal Society. Doing it would hurt. To save myself, I'd do it anyway. I mattered, and I deserved a chance to figure out who I really was.

Squaring my shoulders, I marched up the driveway and front walk. I stopped on the front porch like I had this morning. So much had happened in such a short amount of time. Life felt compressed into a tiny box, and I couldn't escape yet. In less than two hours, I had to trade a key for Drew's life.

The wards shifted and rippled, displaying their silly warning. Mom wouldn't actually have set up wards to kill anyone. She wasn't stupid. Dead bodies on the front porch wouldn't go over well with the neighbors or the cops. The warning would scare off anyone who didn't stop to think it through.

Dispersing the wards would take too long. Mom had pumped too much power into them for simple, obvious strategies to work. Stealing would also take too long. I needed to create a rift in the wards and bring a piece of the outside with me.

Or move so fast the wards couldn't heal the breach. Which I could do if I could slow time on purpose.

So far, I'd done it without understanding how. My fervent wish for more time had created an effect I didn't know how to control. I wished I'd thought to ask Wimahl about it. But I couldn't stop and ask someone every time I needed to do something new. I needed to do it. Less thinking, less worrying, more doing.

For the moment, I decided not to concern myself with whether Mom would notice my actions or not. Any alarms I triggered would either bring her running or not. I'd deal with her when I saw her. One step at a time, keep moving forward. Do things.

I raised a hand and slashed a line of dispersion through the warding. The rift appeared as a writhing blue line with dark flickers. Sticking my other hand into the line, I focused more on dispersion. In a sense, I vibrated the magic apart, sending whispers of power back into the ecosystem. Like sticking a hot poker into a bucket of water.

Once the hole widened enough for me to step through, I squatted and fished the spare key from under the welcome mat. I unlocked the door and pushed it open, still maintaining the rift.

As soon as I stopped maintaining the rift, it would repair itself. I'd have maybe five seconds. Once it repaired itself, I'd lose the ability to use magic until I escaped the house again. I needed more time.

My path had to take me to my parents' bedroom, where I'd have to search for any notes, journals, or diaries my mom kept. If I didn't find anything there, I'd have to ransack the house. At a minimum, I needed ten minutes.

Wait. Did I need magic to do any of this? Only if Mom safeguarded her notes with magic. In her own home, she might not bother. In fact, I suspected she'd avoid doing that because magic attracted attention. Even with my paltry ability to see auras, she wouldn't have wanted to risk me discovering anything by accident. She knew I practiced my aura reading around the house.

Not that all my practice had done me much good.

Focus, Sophie. Run now, rage later. Drew needed me, and even if I didn't have to hurry, we didn't have forever.

I took a deep breath, then I dashed inside the house. Following the path I'd visualized, I darted up the stairs and into the master bedroom. Halfway up the stairs, the wards settled into place. My vision lost sharpness, like I viewed life through a grimy window. The wards clamped down on my ability to use magic, as before and as expected. Magical, invisible bubble wrap surrounded me, grounding my power and blunting my ability to sense Drew or Gabe.

In the master bedroom, I started lifting things and replacing them, looking for papers and notes as if I expected Mom to arrive at any moment and didn't want her to know. But why? Mom knowing I'd gone through her things made no difference to me anymore.

Picking up her jewelry box, I stared at it. Mom cared more about the contents of the box than she did about me.

Well.

No. That wasn't true. She didn't sit and talk to her necklaces while polishing them. We'd never had moments where she'd given the impression the jewelry mattered to her more than anything else.

She cared about me the same as she cared about her jewelry. Her clothes and I held equal status in her life. Unlike, say, my brothers. They knew a different Mom than I did. She loved them as offspring. I'd watched her kiss them goodnight while I got a pat on the head.

I threw the jewelry box across the room. Gold, silver, and gemstones spat across the floor. Rage goaded me to smash perfume bottles against the wall. I tore all the drawers out of the dresser and flung them at the floor.

Within the mess, I spotted a worn, crinkled, leather-bound notebook. I snatched it up and flipped through it. Mom's handwriting? Check. Mention of roses? Check. Diagrams I knew from paying attention at coven meetings? Check.

For good measure, I dashed through the house and basement. I saw no sign of Drew, which meant Mom had more likely taken him to the woods to set up an ambush with him at the center. Good to know.

When I ran out the front door, the wards released me and I breathed freely again. Gabe still waited with the car at the end of the driveway. I laughed. We'd worried about silly things. One piece of my day had gone right, from start to end, and that surprised me so much I laughed with relief.

We still had to rescue Drew, but with this fresh, simple victory, I finally felt like we could win against my mom. She didn't know everything. She couldn't predict everything. She hadn't prepared for everything.

I could win.

CHAPTER 30

Gabe drove. I read the book. First, I opened it to the front to get a feel for how long she'd kept it. None of the pages had dates, though, so I had no idea. The back of the book had ten blank pages left. We still had two hours, so I returned to the beginning and skimmed.

Half an hour later, we sat in the parking lot where we'd picked up the car. I closed the book and set it on my lap, not sure where to start. Mom had left out a lot of stuff she obviously already knew, which made figuring some of it hard. But I definitely knew a few things with certainty that I hadn't known before.

"My mom sent me to the power sink to burn out my witch powers. I thought maybe that might be the case, but now I know it's true. She has a ritual she wants to perform that's spelled out in here," I tapped the book, "and it requires a burned-out witch to use as a conduit. Someone with potential isn't good enough. They have to have gained witch power, then gotten burned out somehow.

"She also needs a source of power she can bring to a site, which explains her interest in the key. And she needs some virgin blood. In this context, it doesn't mean the person who bleeds has to be a virgin, it means the blood can't have interacted with magic before, and her notes say she can use an animal instead of a person."

Funny how I'd thought of that last thing before, the virgin blood. At least I'd been right. It had nothing to do with sex.

"But I have no idea what the ritual is for. There are plenty of mentions of Jenny, which was her sister's name. Her sister died twenty years ago. So what could Jenny possibly have to do with anything?"

Gabe pulled the keys out of the ignition. "Does she need something from a grave or a corpse?"

"No. She needs those three ingredients. Everything else is arrangements and how to feed power. Things like that. I don't quite understand it all because she's using shorthand or code or something that only she understands. Which makes sense, because she didn't expect anyone else to use the notes."

Drumming my fingers on the book, I willed it to help me understand why she would want to hurt me like that. What possible reason could she have found to make me worth more with my power burned out? Like that, I thought I'd still register as magical to everything but have no ability to defend myself at all. If I didn't, then I'd become a regular person.

"Do you want my dad to look over the notes?"

"We've only got an hour left, and we still need to get there and find that spot. Drew got his bearings when we were there before. I didn't."

Gabe opened his door. I followed his lead and dropped the book onto the seat. When he shut the door, he looked at me over the car's roof. "Could she burn out Drew's witch power?"

The bottom fell out of my stomach. If she did that, I'd know it from backlash through the binding, so she hadn't done it yet. But she could. She already had at least one source for rituals.

Then I remembered how Drew had taken those two tokens from my private sanctum to keep them safe. Why hadn't I thought of them before? The first time I considered a battle between Drew and Mom, I'd known it wouldn't end well. This second time, it sounded like an apocalypse-level disaster waiting to happen. For Drew and me, anyway. And also Gabe.

"All the blood just drained out of your face, so I'm going to go with yes." Gabe circled the car, took my hand, and pulled me toward the water. "So we probably shouldn't waste any more time."

I stumbled in his wake, too busy imagining all the ways this could go wrong to notice Wimahl until he put his hands on my shoulders and squeezed. He still wore his swim trunks. His eyes reminded me of a thunderstorm.

"Sophie. You're panicking. I don't know you and I can see that. This isn't a time for panic. This is a time for level-headed rage."

Blinking at him, I thought I'd somehow made time skip forward instead of slowing. "How do we stop her?"

"The same way you stop anyone or anything. With hope, love, and a fierce belief that you're doing the right thing."

I kept staring. He sounded like a character in a cheesy fantasy movie.

"Dad, can you tell us how someone might burn out a witch?"

Wimahl frowned. "It takes power. A lot of power. The burner has to overcome the victim's defenses, then flood them with more power than they could ever handle. The mechanics of it is simple. The execution is the hard part."

"But that won't work on Drew." Had my mom made a critical mistake in taking Drew? Hope flickered in my chest. "He can shunt excess power to me, Gabe, and the node. There's no bottom to that well, it just keeps filling."

"Then her first step will likely involve an attempt to cut off those links, either permanently or temporarily. She's probably been making that attempt while you've been running around after this key in your coat pocket. If I were you, I'd get moving and go interrupt that as fast as you can." Wimahl pushed me toward the water.

"Any tips for finding her?" Gabe took my hand again, keeping me moving.

"You're bound to Drew. Use that. And she's doing something big. If you can't see that from a fair distance away, you might as well give up now."

I didn't need to hear it phrased like that. "Can you come help us?"

"There isn't much I can do, as constrained as I am. I have faith in you, though. Wrap your arms around Gabriel's neck and go save your friend."

Gabe helped me jump onto his back, then he dove into the water. The rhythm of his body moving helped me calm down. So did the water. Plunging into this strange other world before facing my insane mom helped me center. It helped me orient on what mattered.

Drew. Gabe. Me. All of us wanted to live our lives and not deal with pressure forced on us by the outside. Gabe had an amazing dad who wanted to help us all do that. No one else seemed interested in letting us grow and discover the world on our own terms.

I wished I could've met Gabe's dad so much earlier. I also wished I'd thought to ask him about affecting time. Again. Nothing for it but to do what I could do and learn about it later.

This time, if we got Drew back without stopping Mom, I'd make him take us to Claire. With the combined force of everyone at her disposal, we could defeat Mom for good. Hopefully, it wouldn't come to killing her. At this point, though, if I had to choose between Mom and anyone else I knew, I'd choose the other person.

If I had to choose between Mom and me, I'd choose...me. Yes, I'd choose myself. She didn't deserve my hesitation, my loyalty, or anything else from me except disgust. Abducting Drew to force me to help her perform some ritual, even if it would save the world from something worse than anything ever seen before, earned her whatever she got.

Between one breath and another, everything blanked and I stood inside the cabin again. Immediately, I knew no one had pulled me into my private sanctum or home because Drew leaned his back against the door.

The leaves in his private sanctum glowed with soft green light. His walls, made from lively, vibrant wood, rippled with a silver sheen. Where my door had a crappy latch, his had a deadbolt, a steel bar across it, and a lever in the wall.

Drew smiled at me and didn't show any signs of distress. "Hey, Sophie. How are things going for you? Your aura looks different. Smoother."

"Why am I here?"

His smile deepened to a grin. "Your mom is trying so very hard to get inside. She seems to think that having me under her physical control equates to having me under her mental control, and that's really not how things work. I'm not unconscious, she only thinks I am. Even if I was, I have solid passive defenses." He patted the bar on the door.

The cabin shook. I braced myself between the bed and the wall.

"I'm a tiny bit worried because she can do that." He pointed over his shoulder with his thumb. "So I called you here just in case. I don't seem to be able to do anything else, aside from taking all the power you keep shunting to me."

While I blinked at him like an idiot, Drew stuck his hand in his pocket and retrieved four tokens. I recognized my two blue ones. Another had a green shimmer over blue that probably represented his link with Claire. The fourth was rose shaped for Portland. He offered them to me on his open palm.

"These are important. On the chance she somehow gets through, you need to keep them safe from here. With these all in your possession, it'll also make shunting her power to you easier in my current state."

I took the tokens and nodded. As I'd trusted him, he now trusted me. "Which will make it even harder for her to break in."

"Hopefully, yes."

Dozens of things ran through my head to tell him, about Gabe's mom, Wimahl, the new magic things I'd learned, and my mom.

"Are you on your way to rescue me?" He sounded so calm.

"Yes. We have the second key. Hold on as long as you can, okay?" I hugged him. "Just hold on. We'll save you."

"You're doing great. I know you are." He squeezed me. When I let go, he gave me a swift, chaste kiss. "Good luck."

"You too." I touched my mouth and left him to defend himself so Gabe and I could rescue him.

CHAPTER 31

By the time Gabe walked out of the water in the fading sunlight, my panic had dissipated. I hopped off his back. He pulled the water out of my clothes and hair. Instead of letting it fall into the Columbia River, he kept it hovering in the air alongside us.

"You know what? I think I'm going to use this as armor. Because who knows what your mom is going to do to us. And enough water to encase someone might come in handy."

"I like your plan." Mine didn't involve anything so concrete—save Drew, stop Mom, survive.

"Thanks." The water surrounded him as if it had a membrane holding it in a shell the same shape as his body. "I'm not used to this binding with you guys, but I think Drew is that way." He pointed into the woods.

"Now that you mention it, yeah." I saw my link to Drew disappearing in that direction. Sometimes, things worked out better than I expected. Thank goodness.

As ready as I'd ever be, I jogged with Gabe to find Drew.

Faint, flickering blue surrounded a wide area. As soon as I saw it, I knew we had the right place. Inside it, I caught sight of movement. I patted Gabe's arm and pointed for us to hide so we could watch before plunging into an unknown situation. And so I could mess with Mom's ward, barrier, or whatever she'd made, out of sight.

We slipped behind a fallen log with as little noise as we could manage. I gestured for Gabe to watch while I focused on the magic.

"Tell me if she seems to notice what I'm doing," I whispered.

He nodded and peeled the water from his face.

As I'd done at home, I reached for the blue dome. There, I'd dispersed, and that had worked. I had a feeling this one involved an alarm. Mom wanted the key. She wouldn't want to keep Gabe and me out.

Strike that—she wouldn't want to keep me out. Gabe, she probably would prefer not to see again.

Dispersing seemed too easy to defeat an alarm. This needed a more complex solution. I needed to cut through the wall without the magic realizing I'd cut through it. Like sticking a chewing gum wrapper or piece of aluminum in the building alarm circuit to keep it from going off. Only with magic.

I needed to convince the wall that it formed around a rock where no rock existed, and I needed to do it fast. No pressure.

"She's moving Drew," Gabe whispered. "Propping him up against a tree. I think he's unconscious."

Mom wouldn't wake up Drew unless she needed to. She knew he could do a lot on his own and probably suspected we could communicate somehow through our bindings.

"Now that I'm ready," Mom said with an edge of annoyance, "you and I are going to have a little chat, you disgusting abomination. I know you seduced my daughter, and you're going to pay for that."

I tried not to listen while I thought about how to craft my solution to Mom's alarm. The moment I thought I had a good idea, raw, scorching power spiraled down my link with Drew. Dropping everything else, I worked to disperse as much as I could and shunt the rest to the node. Gabe grunted, so he felt it too.

Mom had decided to try burning Drew. She wouldn't succeed.

Wait. I had all this power coming from Mom, and I shoved it away from me? I had things I could do with that power. Brushing a fingertip on Mom's wall, I stole that power and used it to change the edge into a new shape.

Gabe said nothing. Mom hadn't noticed.

Take that, Mom. The useless, waste of effort disappointment who couldn't resist you this morning bypassed your stupid alarm with your own stupid power.

I patted Gabe on the shoulder and directed him through the gap I'd created. We crept closer. An old tree stump provided us cover thirty feet from Mom. Drew sat in a messy heap against a trunk. Mom staggered back from him, lowering her arms and panting.

Since I'd used Mom's aura the most to practice seeing magic, I could tell she'd spent herself dry trying to fry Drew. She'd tapped a ley line, though. I saw her replenishing with each passing moment. That meant I didn't have a chance to catch her with her magic pants down.

"Where are you sending it all?" Mom screeched. She stormed to the leafless rosebush, taking her maybe ten feet from Drew. "I will make this work, Jenny! After all this time, today is definitely the day. I swear it on your grave!"

Gabe darted to the next tree, moving closer to Drew while Mom had her back to us.

Inspired by him, I hustled to a different tree. Mom turned. She saw me. I saw her. We stared at each other for a weird, timeless moment.

My heart ramped up to eighty miles an hour. I hadn't put a lot of thought into how this moment would go and didn't know what to do. My entire focus had settled on finding Drew and stopping Mom without a lot of consideration for how to make those two things happen.

Mom smiled like she genuinely wanted to see me. "Sophie. I wasn't expecting you yet."

Surprise? That sweet smile confused me. Did she think I'd strolled up that moment and heard nothing she'd screamed five seconds earlier? "Didn't want to keep you waiting."

"You're such a good girl. Give me the key." She held out her hand.

The gall of her. "Wake Drew and let him go." I held out my hand like she could hand him over as an annoyed echo of her gesture. My dumb hand shook.

Mom's smile evaporated. "You always have to do things the hard way. It's not enough that I take care of you—"

"Shut up, Belinda." Shaking from head to toe, I took a step toward her. Claire would do this. I wanted to be more like Claire, and this fit her well. "I don't care. Release Drew and you can have your stupid key." What would I do once she had the key? No idea. Rush her, maybe? Hope for Drew and Gabe to save my bacon? Ack?

She looked like she'd swallowed a lemon. "Sit."

Power swirled around her and reached for me. Not this time, Mom. I slashed a hand through the air, using the gesture to focus my own power on dispersing hers.

Mom flinched. She hadn't expected me to fight back. Or she hadn't expected me to succeed.

"I'm not your dog, Belinda."

Peering at me, Mom narrowed her eyes. "He's sending the power to you."

Crap, she'd started figuring things out. I needed a distraction. The first time we'd found her in this spot, mentioning Claire's dad had tripped her up. Another dead person might work the same. "Did you kill Aunt Jenny out here?"

She sucked in a breath like a bellows. "How dare you?" The full force of her angry regard carried a palpable weight. Staying there took a heap of courage bolstered by the knowledge Gabe would back me up. "You don't know anything about what happened to Jenny."

Out of the corner of my eye, I noticed Gabe's watery form slipping closer to Drew. He might have luck freeing Drew from whatever coercions

Mom had him under. Any time I could give him meant a better chance Drew would wake up and help me out of this mess. "For all I know, you lured her out here, chopped her up, and buried her under this rosebush for daring to smile at your boyfriend."

The sharp slap she delivered with magic took me by surprise. My new passive shields absorbed some of the blow. What got through snapped my head to the side.

"I didn't kill my sister!" Mom stormed at me, her hands balling into fists. "She played with things she didn't understand and couldn't control. She was like you! Weak and stupid."

I stumbled backward because I didn't want her touching me again.

"Always pushing, always trying to do things she couldn't. She did that to herself!" Mom stabbed a finger at the rosebush. "I've been trying to save her for twenty years. Then you came along. And you're perfect for this, sweetie." Reaching toward me, she let the rage melt from her expression, replaced by her usual attempt at motherly concern. That attempt had fooled me for a long time, probably because I'd never seen anything else.

She clasped her hands like a princess pleased to see her pony. "You can't do anything worthwhile with your power. You don't need it. I wanted to show you, to tell you why your sacrifice matters."

Taking another step back, I forced myself not to check on Gabe and Drew. My eyes flicking over there once would tip off Mom. "What sacrifice? Why does it matter? I don't understand. I want to." And I did. Sort of. I wanted to escape more than I cared about Mom's demented problems.

"Jenny." Mom sighed and waved at the enormous rosebush. "She's trapped inside the plant. You can give her new life, let her roam free."

Wait. What?

"Your powers are so minimal, they don't matter. With my help, you'd be free too. Both of you could have the normal life you deserve."

"Jenny. Your little sister who died when she was twelve. Is in that plant." I couldn't make any of those bizarre things into a question with Mom gazing at me like I'd offered myself to her as a Christmas present.

"Her soul, yes. Don't you see? I've only ever wanted to help you both." Mom offered me her hand. She apparently thought this sounded enticing instead of repulsive.

I covered my mouth to hide my desire to vomit. "How did it happen?"

"She wanted so badly to help with the roses for the festival. So I let her come with me to help." Mom's wistful sigh sounded like real regret. "But I didn't know Laura Marius had found my special project out here. I was experimenting with color-shifting petals. When I found her, with Jenny in tow, we shouted at each other. Laura and I dueled, but it wasn't a big deal. Jenny tried to help. In the confusion..."

Mom sighed again. "She tried to control too much power and do something too complicated. It killed her body. The magic flying around and the enchantments already on the plant combined to snare her soul. If she'd just stayed out of it, she would've been fine."

Nothing like blaming the victim for your own mistakes. Like she'd done to me, over and over.

"But I finally found the perfect ritual to help Jenny. Then you had to go and meet that boy." Her anger returned. She jabbed her finger at Drew and turned enough to see Gabe crouched beside him, slowly covering Drew's body with water. "No!"

Mom moved faster than I could process. She wrapped her hand around my neck and pulled a knife out of who knew where. "Get away from him, Gabe, or I'll slit Sophie's throat." She held the blade against my skin.

Gabe raised his hands in surrender and stood. His water remained in place, covering Drew's lower body. "She's your daughter."

"That's right. She's mine. Give me the key. Right now."

Stunned by Mom's unexpected change of tactics and the knife at my neck, I met Gabe's gaze. He didn't know what to do either. I could see it in his eyes.

Options, I needed options. If Mom stabbed me, Gabe could heal me, but only if he got to me in time and didn't have to do anything else. Slowing time might net me a less serious cut, which would increase my chances of survival a lot. Other possibilities...

I had one. A crazy one.

CHAPTER 32

With Mom's focus on Gabe, I reached for power from the node. My well couldn't hold much, but I could keep that connection open. The node could flood me faster than Mom's ley line could replenish her.

"It's in my coat pocket," I said. Pay no attention to Sophie's preparations.

"Get it and hold it up where I can reach it."

Mom had two hands and two teenagers to worry about. She'd realize that too. I had to do something she wouldn't expect.

I dug out the key and held it up. We all stood still. Mom shifted her weight, and I had a feeling she thought about cutting me. A good injury would keep me docile and prove her intent.

So I launched a preemptive attack. A magical attack. One designed to force us into a duel. I didn't think I could win against Mom by myself. She wouldn't believe I could win one either. But I didn't have to win. Gabe only needed a minute or two to free Drew. Then they could both charge to my rescue.

Because this wasn't about me. It was about us. I had friends, and they would back me up. Mom had...a possessed rosebush, I guess?

Around us, leaves exploded into life, the ground churned under the dead leaves, the dusting of snow melted, the mud dried, and the sun blasted to high noon on a clear day. Mom and I faced each other with a normal-sized rosebush to my right and a ring of sapphire cushions to my left.

Mom blinked at me, no longer holding a knife. "What did you do?" She seemed more puzzled than outraged.

"This is it? This is your sanctum? This is where you consider home? Do none of us matter to you at all? I thought you cared about your sons, at least."

Her mouth twisted into a snarl. "How did you do this?" She held out her hands and blasted a jet of sky blue water at me.

I rolled to the side and focused on my shields. Keeping her busy meant letting her shoot as much as she wanted. "The only person you care about is a dead girl?"

"You can't do any of this. You're weak! You don't have enough power to spark a lightbulb!"

She blasted. I ducked and rolled. Deciding I cared more about me than her had given me a kind of freedom. The words coming out of her mouth didn't hurt anymore. She didn't matter.

"What were you even doing out here before, when we stumbled into you?"

"I should've burned out your power right away. Letting you keep it was a mistake. But Anne thought you'd contribute well enough. She thought you had a purpose."

Blah, blah, blah. At least I knew Anne had kind of stood up for me at some point. We could talk later, and she could explain why she went along with Mom's plan. Somehow, I suspected I'd hear about how Mom seemed so desperate or obsessed, or something like that.

"You were setting up a second try at burning me out, weren't you? Only we interrupted you, and then you saw the key."

"And Drew ruined everything! How did you get through that power sink intact?"

I snorted at her. "Drew. Duh."

She blasted again. This time, I set my feet, held out my hands, and stole from her. The blast funneled through me to Drew.

Maybe I didn't need a rescue after all. Mom didn't have enough power to break me. Not anymore. In a way, I'd already won this battle. I'd made my choices.

Screaming her impotent rage, Mom tried to blast me harder, except she didn't have any more power to fling.

"You're exhausting yourself for no reason, Belinda." I wanted to finish this. Time slowed for me so I could do something I'd never tried before without hurting myself.

Instead of siphoning the power to Drew, I held it, changed it, and reflected it. For her, it happened so fast she didn't see anything in time to react. The blast hit her in the face.

Mom dropped. The attack stopped. I'd won. What would I do? When Mom had invaded my private sanctum, she'd ransacked it. If I wanted to, I could do the same. I could find her link to the Petal Society and break it. Anything she wanted to keep secret from me, I could discover.

But I wouldn't. Because I didn't want to, and because the idea of it disgusted me. Doing those things to her wouldn't make me stronger. It'd make me as weak and awful as her. Defeat didn't have to mean destruction.

I'd never won a duel before. As I stood over my mom, wondering how to leave the metaphysical space, I noticed thin, weak threads holding me there. With a thought, I severed them.

I hit the ground harder than expected and lost my balance. My butt hit the ground. Mom scrabbled across the ground, frantic for something. She picked up the key.

Gabe shouted. I blinked like a moron. Mom pulled out the box and smashed the key against it.

Maybe, thought a piece of me, I shouldn't have slowed time in a metaphysical battle to spare myself some pain while fumbling through something new so I could save that option for right after when Mom did something crazy.

Nothing I could do would stop the box opening. I lurched to my feet and ran to Gabe. Drew remained unconscious, because of course he did. Gabe hadn't covered his entire body. Leaving his face free so he could breathe hadn't broken the magical hold Mom had placed. I could've told him that wouldn't work fast enough.

I took one of Drew's arms. Gabe got the idea and took the other. We hauled him around the tree and farther away from Mom.

Gross yellow light, the color of bile-heavy vomit, spilled from the box. Mom held it over her head in triumph and pointed the opening at her mouth. She swallowed the gross stuff, letting it engorge her. Yellow overwhelmed her aura.

We hid behind a boulder. Gabe and I watched.

Mom seemed to realize she might have made a mistake, because she let go of the box. It hovered in place. She closed her mouth. The power kept swelling her aura like a balloon. Her eyes widened. Batting at the box did nothing.

Though I wanted to feel like I should save her, I had no reason to. Whatever this box did, she caused the damage to herself.

"What's happening?" Gabe asked.

"I don't think the box holds what she thought."

Mom's aura burst. I ducked. Gabe followed my lead. Force blew out in every direction, throwing downed tree limbs, dead leaves, and a circular spray of mud and small rocks.

When it seemed safe again, I popped my head up and saw Mom lying on the ground, not moving.

Drew groaned. "I'm going to kill her so hard her ghost doesn't rise for a month," he grumbled as he rubbed the back of his head.

"I don't think you'll have to," Gabe said.

"She tried to fight me," Drew growled. "Even with me crippled by her crap, she couldn't do it. It's good to have friends on your side, especially when one's a node."

I needed to know. Leaving the boys behind, I crept toward my mom. She lay so still, I worried about her. The fact that I cared gnawed at me. Mom had no right to make me care.

Her chest rose and fell. Strange yellow spots ringed with thin black ovals covered her exposed flesh. They reminded me of some of the diseases that infected roses. We'd battled them together in the garden every spring. In her quest for the power to save her sister, Mom had infected herself with some kind of magical rose blight locked away by people who probably had no idea how to destroy it.

They'd put one key into a trap no sane witch would try to defeat and no nonmagical person would see. The other key had gone under the protection of a witch who hadn't realized what it did.

As I closed the distance, I gradually realized something was missing. Mom had no aura.

She didn't have a constrained or shrunken aura—she had nothing. Not a trace of magic lingered and clung to her. The woman who'd spent so much time and effort dominating me with her power had lost it all.

I nudged her with my shoe. "Mom?"

She groaned. "Is Jenny free?" Of course she asked about the object of her twenty-year obsession.

"No. But since it's clear she needs help, I'll take care of it."

Mom opened her eyes and glared at me. "You little brat." Her mouth stopped moving. Her eyes widened. She knew. She'd tried to do something with magic, probably to affect me, and discovered she had nothing.

Seeing her discover her loss made me queasy. On one hand, I relished her distress. I hated her and wanted her to suffer. On the other, she was still my mom and a person. My anger won, for the most part. "We have a burned-out witch now. How does the ritual work?"

Sitting up, Mom held out her hands and turned them over. She blinked a lot and said nothing.

Maybe we'd just get Claire to deal with it.

CHAPTER 33

Drew took Gabe and me home by shifting us with his power. We left Mom in the forest because none of us wanted to deal with her. The moment we stepped into the haven Claire had created for her family and friends, I hugged myself. Sunshine warmed us and laughter rang in the trees of a forest similar to the one we'd left. Claire stepped into sight as if summoned.

She had dark hair, olive-toned Mediterranean-kissed skin, and a warm, welcoming smile. "How'd your witch thing go? Is it time to charge in and save the day, or did you all take care of that on your own?"

Drew stepped to her side and slid an arm around her waist. She kissed his cheek.

I beamed at her and wanted to spend the rest of the day doing nothing more than watching her do things. Anything. Reading a book, holding Drew, eating, staring at the trees, anything. Claire was a goddess to me.

"Hi, I'm Gabriel. People call me Gabe. You must be Claire. I'm Sophie's friend and part of the coven."

Claire and Gabe shook hands. "Nice to meet you, Gabe."

Gabe nudged me. I blushed. And said nothing. I could stand up to my mom and say terrible things to her, but could I even greet Claire? No.

"We do have a tiny problem with a possessed rosebush," Drew said. "But it can wait. Sophie's mom maybe should be handled as soon as possible.

She's got some kind of magical curse, and it might be infectious."

"Oh, no, I don't think so." Words flooded from me in a stupid rush. "She doesn't have an aura anymore, so nothing can interact with it. Someone would have to prod the blight on purpose, and the coven deserves to be infected by it if they're stupid enough to do that."

Claire crinkled her nose. I wanted to kiss it. "Isn't Anne part of the coven? I know we're not best pals or anything, but we should probably help her out enough so she doesn't have to suffer that."

"Maybe you and Sophie could go check it out," Gabe said. "See if there's any easy intervention options."

I wanted to hug him and murder him at the same time.

"Maybe I should go too." Drew looked as distressed as I felt.

"Nah, the ladies can handle it." Gabe draped an arm around Drew's shoulders. "There's no real threat anymore, and if there is, it's a ghost. That's Claire's department."

Claire let go of Drew and offered me her hand. "Sure. If you're up to it, Sophie? I can get us there and back."

"Oh. Um. Okay! I guess. I mean, I suppose we shouldn't let Mom die out there. In the cold. Without a coat. Maybe." I took Claire's hand and hoped she didn't notice my pulse speed to a zillion miles an hour. Her fingers had callouses from practicing with her dagger, a magical blade I'd helped enchant an eon—one week, which felt like forever—ago.

Gabe flashed me a grin as he steered Drew elsewhere, the jerk.

In a flash, we shifted back to the swiftly darkening forest. Mom stumbled away from us, disappearing into the distance. I thought I heard her crying.

"She's up and moving, so I think she'll be okay." Claire stared at the rosebush without me prompting her. "Yep, it's possessed. Let me see if I can release the ghost so we can put it to rest properly." She slid her dagger from its sheath at her side. The blade, as long as her forearm, had a curve like a giant tooth or claw, and the guard resembled bat-like wings. "Worst case, I destroy the ghost and that's that."

While she approached the enormous plant, I leaned against a tree. My mouth opened, and I told her everything that had happened. She didn't need to know all of it, but I had to say these things to someone and didn't know who else to trust. Drew and Gabe already knew all the biggest parts, so telling them made no difference.

She sliced canes off various parts of the rosebush while I spoke. By the time I finished, she'd hacked off enough to reveal a root ball. "Sounds like you had a rough week today."

I chuckled. "You could say that."

"You know you're welcome to stay with us as long as you want, right?"

"Yes. Thank you."

She lunged at the plant and stabbed the root ball. High-pitched squealing hurt my ears. I covered them and watched white mist stream upward to form a vague, writhing mass. Though I'd seen ghosts before, I'd never seen one this close.

"Is it dangerous?"

"We're going to watch it for ten minutes or so to figure that out." She held her dagger ready for action at a moment's notice.

I struggled to figure out how I felt about her. My heart wanted to sit and talk to her forever. Or lie in bed, sharing warmth and feeling safe. I wished her smile counted as an invitation. Wanting these things with a girl still confused me. Further, wanting them with both Claire and Drew at the same time made me blush. Speaking of Claire's boyfriend...

"Drew said some stuff." Look at me, the fierce mom-defeater who couldn't muster the courage to talk about a real issue with real people who mattered.

"I'm sure he did. Talking is one of his things. I'm guessing it was about something other than calculus or you wouldn't mention it."

"Um. He said, I mean, I was dying, so I don't know if he meant it.

Maybe he just wanted me to think—" I gulped and faced her. Gabe was right. I felt something for her—and for Drew—that my screwed-up family hadn't prepared me for. She deserved my honesty. "He told me he loved me."

Claire glanced at me, her expression inscrutable, then she returned to her vigilant watch of the unmoving ghost. "Yes, he does."

I blinked like an idiot and had to grope for words. "You knew that? And you're not upset?"

"No, I'm not upset." She shrugged. One corner of her mouth quirked into a smile. "He's had a lot of loss and pain in his life. The more he can open himself to other people, the less chance he'll take all that power he commands and become a monster. Besides, I like having you in that cabin with us."

My pulse thudded in my ears. Leaving Mom had given me the best family imaginable. "You do?"

"Yes." She glanced at me again and cracked a full grin. "Sophie, you're not in the way or keeping us from messing around. We're pretty happy with how things are, and that includes you. Love isn't sex, and sex isn't love." Keeping an eye on the ghost, she returned to my side and draped an arm around my shoulders.

She smelled like pine needles and sunshine. "I'm sorry things didn't work out with your mom, but only because I know what it's like to lose your family. The part where that means you stay with us is pretty awesome."

I didn't know what to say. We stood together and watched the ghost writhe above the plant. My heart rate slowed to normal as I reveled in Claire's closeness. When I let my gaze stray to her, to drink in the shape of her nose and chin, she glanced at me. I blushed and looked away.

Claire had Drew. She didn't need me for anything more than friendship. I'd be fine.

She sheathed her dagger. "This ghost isn't going anywhere for now. I'll come back later and check on it."

"Okay."

Neither of us moved.

"I'd like to ask you something, but I'm not sure how you feel about stuff like that. And really, I'm not sure how I feel about it either." Claire withdrew her arm and put her hands on my shoulders. She turned me to face her.

I stared at her with no idea what to expect. Nothing in her expression gave me a clue I could decipher.

"Is it okay..." She blushed. My hero's cheeks actually darkened. "...if I kiss you?"

"What?" My brain ceased to function.

Claire let go and looked at the ground. "Never mind. I just had this idea—" She shrugged and didn't finish.

"What idea?" Did I gush? I thought I gushed, breathless with a glorious rush of something confusing and amazing.

She glanced at me, then shook her head. "It's nothing."

All this time, I'd considered her the boldest, most confident person in the universe, able to do anything, stand up to anyone, and punch anything in the face. I'd put her on a marble pedestal and worshiped her as a remote hero, too incredible to touch. But I was wrong.

Claire needed us as much as we needed her.

I gulped, shaken by the revelation. My hero didn't stride like a goddess, above the fray of confusion and uncertainty. She had doubts and fears like me. Drew had tried to tell me as much, but I hadn't believed him.

All my life, everyone had more than me. More power, more confidence, more authority, more something. I'd never considered the possibility I could qualify as their equal.

And she asked! No one asked my permission for anything. They took what they wanted. I kind of let them.

No, I completely let them. My coven, the women who should have taught me how to stand up for myself, had pushed me down and treated me like a doormat. So I'd become one.

Not anymore.

"It's not nothing." My heart beat several zillion times per second. Heat burned my cheeks so hard I thought my head might explode.

If she could ask, if she could use the words, then so could I. Trying with all my might to not gasp for breath, I said, "Can you kiss me? Yes! Please."

Claire looked up and smiled like I'd surprised her. She touched my cheek with her thumb, brushing stray hairs from my face.

I took her other hand and squeezed it.

She kissed me. Time slowed, or maybe it stopped. I felt like a partner, not a follower. Claire didn't pity me or consider me a burden.

I didn't know how this would end, but I sure knew how it began. With love.

Other Books by Lee French

Spirit Knights

Girls Can't Be Knights

Backyard Dragons

Ethereal Entanglements

Ghost Is the New Normal

Boys Can't Be Witches

War of the Rose Covens

Death and Dragons In Omaha (coming 2020)

Harper Revolution

Defiance (coming late 2019)

Porcelain

Crawlspace

Maze Beset trilogy

Dragons In Pieces

Dragons In Chains

Dragons In Flight

Superheroes in Denim (compilation)

WWW.AUTHORLEEFRENCH.COM

Fantasy in the Ilauris setting

Damsel In Distress

Shadow & Spice (short story)

Al-Kabar

The Greatest Sin

(with Erik Kort)

The Fallen

Harbinger

Moon Shades

Illusive Echoes

A Curse of Memories

Darkside Seattle

Street Doc

Fixer

Mechanic

Hacker

Meat (coming in 2019)

Anthology Appearances

Merely This and Nothing More: Poe Goes Punk

Unnatural Dragons: a science fiction anthology

What We've Unlearned: English Class Goes Punk

Hideous Progeny: Horror Goes Punk

Enter the Aftermath

Undercurrents: What Lies Beneath

Swords, Sorcery, & Self-Rescuing Damsels

About the Author

Lee French is a USA TODAY bestselling author living in Olympia, WA, with two kids, two bicycles, and too much stuff. She is an avid gamer and a member of the Myth-Weavers online RPG community. In addition to spending too much time there, she also trains in taekwondo, keeps a nice flower garden with one dragon and absolutely no lawn gnomes, works an excessive number of book events, and tries in vain every year to grow vegetables that don't get devoured by neighborhood wildlife.

She is an active member of the Science Fiction and Fantasy Writers of America and the Northwest Independent Writers Association, as well as serving the Olympia region as a NaNoWriMo Municipal Liaison.